YESTERDAY

Book One of the Yesterday Series

A Novel By

Amanda Tru

Published by
Sign of the Whale Books™

PUBLISHED BY: *Sign of the Whale Books™**, an imprint of *Olivia Kimbrell Press™*, P.O. Box 4393, Winchester, KY 40392-4393. The *Sign of the Whale Books™* colophon and Icthus/spaceship/whale logo are trademarks of *Olivia Kimbrell Press™*.
*Sign of the Whale Books™ is an imprint specializing in Biblical and/or Christian fiction primarily with fantasy, magical, speculative fiction, futuristic, science fiction, and/or other supernatural themes.

Original Copyright © 2012.

Cover Art and Graphics by Debi Warford (www.debiwarford.com)

Library Cataloging Data
Tru, Amanda (Amanda Tru) 1978-

  Yesterday, book 1 in the Yesterday Series/Amanda Tru
    197 p. 20.32cm x 12.7cm (8in x 5in.)

Summary: Hannah has the ability to time travel but there are consequences. After saving a family injured in a car accident, Hannah wakes the next morning to find her yesterday was five years ago!

    ISBN: 978-1-939603-67-8

1. time travel 2. christian romantic mystery 3. new adult 4. male and female relationships 5. parodoxes

[PS3568.AW475 M328 2012]
248.8'43 — dc211

YESTERDAY

Book One of the Yesterday Series

A Novel By

Amanda Tru

TABLE OF CONTENTS

DEDICATION

For my sisters.

For Cami, who inspired me to write it in the first place,
and for Janna, who inspired me to keep writing and finish.

And for Him. Psalm 139

CHAPTER ONE

RED flashed against the bright white of the snow.

I slammed on the brakes. The SUV skidded toward the guardrail.

My heart seemed to stop. I couldn't breathe. My body felt suspended as the mountainous terrain whirled across my vision. I braced for impact. Unexpectedly, the vehicle lurched as the tires found traction and came to a sudden stop

I sucked in air. My eyes frantically searched the heavy snowfall.

What had I seen?

Was it human?

Had I hit something?

The Sierra mountains were shrouded in the stillness of the winter storm, silent and revealing no secrets. Had I just imagined something dart in front of me?

I caught a glimpse of a fist out of the corner of my eye. I jumped. A strangled scream escaped my throat as the fist started hammering on my window. Heart thumping, I peered beyond the relentless pounding to see the outline of a woman in a red parka. She was screaming, but I couldn't understand her words.

Fingers fumbling and shaking, I rolled down my window. At her appearance, an electric current of shock ripped through me.

Blood streamed from somewhere on her head. It trickled down to her chin, leaving a dark red trail. Dirty tears streaked her cheeks, and her hair hung in clumps of frizzy knots.

I frantically jerked open my door.

"Are you okay?" I asked.

But she didn't answer. Instead, she continued to scream, her hysterical cries now slicing through me.

"Help! Help! Please help me! I can't get them out!"

What was she talking about? My eyes traced an invisible line to where she was gesturing. A few yards in front of my own fender, the meager guardrail was bent and scraped. Peering through the falling snow, I could see beyond that to where the frozen earth had been torn up. Standing on the frame of my car door, I looked into the embankment off the side. Red tail lights glowed like beacons.

The shock to my senses was like a physical blow. I sprang out of the car, stepping into a blood stained patch of snow. Blood had dripped from the woman's leg where her torn pants exposed a jagged wound. Her sobbing and frantic cries continued, but she wasn't making sense.

Her skin was chalky green. She was in shock, yet I felt paralyzed. My medical background consisted of a three hour CPR and first aid class I'd taken over a year ago. Panic washed over me like a wave. I didn't know how to help her!

Desperate, I gently pushed her toward the back seat of the SUV. Her feet shuffled forward two steps, and then she collapsed. I caught her around the shoulders and practically dragged her rag doll frame.

She roused enough to help as I lifted her into the back seat. I unraveled the scarf from my neck and wrapped it around her leg above the bloody gash, tying it as tightly as I could.

Reaching into the back of the SUV, I located a large flashlight and my old coat that I used when skiing. I wrapped the arms of the coat loosely around her leg, hoping the bulky material would soak up some of the blood.

"What's your name?" I asked the woman.

She cleared her throat and shook her head, her brow creasing with confusion. Instead, she began a new litany of faint but frantic cries about her family.

"You can tell me later. I'm Hannah."

"Help! My family… !"

"I'm going down into the ravine right now. Stay here. I'll help them. I promise."

Hoping I didn't just make a promise I couldn't keep, I shut the door and tripped my way through the snowdrifts toward the red haloed taillights.

I pulled my phone out of my coat pocket. There usually wasn't cell phone coverage on this road. But, just maybe…

No service.

This wasn't supposed to be happening! I should be at my sister's lodge at the top of the mountain not crawling down a steep embankment to help accident victims!

It wasn't even supposed to be snowing! I'd checked the weather report at least a dozen times: no new snow for the next week. Now it was practically a blizzard!

I took deep breaths, trying to control the panic and adrenaline running through my veins as I half climbed, half slid down the incline. This wasn't me. I'm not the brave sort. In fact, I'm pretty much a wimp!

I was facing the risk of a serious panic attack even before any of this had happened. The rational part of my brain said my fear was ridiculous. The roads were supposed to be clear. I'd driven to Silver Springs many times before. And, I was driving the biggest, meanest, previously-owned SUV an over-protective father could buy for his college-age daughter. Despite my best rationale, my hands were sweating, my heart was beating erratically, and I was still at the bottom of the mountain.

But those symptoms were nothing compared to what I experienced now. When my eyes collided with the blue sedan at the bottom, I wanted to turn around and run. The front of the car was wrapped around a tree. How could anyone survive an accident like this?

The gas station attendant's ramblings from earlier replayed in my head like a bad movie. Something about a tragic accident on this same road five years ago. The family had all died.

Taking a deep breath, I felt renewed determination run through my veins as it hitched a ride on an abundance of adrenaline. I had to do this.

"Hello, can anyone hear me?" I called as I slid the last few feet to the bottom of the ravine. My wrist scraped over some exposed branches on the way down, but the pain didn't register. I called again, louder.

No answer.

I didn't want to do this! I didn't want to see the scene inside the mangled car. I drew in a shaky, hiccuping breath.

Reaching the driver's side door, I shined the flashlight inside. The beam flickered in my shaking hand. I counted three passengers, motionless and unresponsive to the bright light. My stomach flipped as the beam caught blood marring each pale face.

I bent over, hyperventilating and gasping for breath. I couldn't do this! They were probably already dead! I closed my eyes. "Please, God, I can't do this! Help me!"

I released my breath slowly, then quickly swung my flashlight back inside before I lost my nerve.

The driver must be the injured woman's husband. In the back seat were two children. The girl I guessed to be about 7; the boy about 5. Though I put all my weight into it, neither door on the driver's side would budge.

I rushed around to the other side, climbing into the mom's empty seat. Reaching into the back seat and searching for the girl's pulse, I sighed in relief. She was alive — unconscious, but with a strong pulse. I climbed further over the seats and reached for the boy. Another pulse! New energy and determination surged through my veins.

Finally, I leaned over to the dad for a pulse. But I

already knew the answer. The front driver's side had taken most of the impact. No one could survive in his position. To my surprise, I felt a slight bump against my finger. It was very faint, but the man was alive… at least for now.

I tried to focus. What could I do? I could drive to the lodge and get my sister, Abby, and her husband, Tom, to come help. We could use the phone at the lodge to call for medical assistance. Then we could get some of the other lodgers, come back and…

I shivered, feeling the freezing cold seep through my coat. It would be too late. I closed my eyes. A sob of fear and frustration caught in my throat. We wouldn't make it back in time. They couldn't survive their injuries or these temperatures for very long. I couldn't leave them. It was all up to me.

I tried not to think. I tried not to feel. I just acted.

The door by the girl opened easily. I unbuckled her seatbelt, took a deep breath, and hoisted her in my arms. She stirred and moaned slightly.

"I've got you. You're going to be alright," I cooed softly as I struggled through the drifts and still-falling snow back up the ravine.

My arms burned with the effort and my labored breathing came in short gasps. Just when I thought I couldn't take another step, I finally reached the SUV. Gently, I placed the girl in the back seat beside her mother.

"Maddie!" The sobbing woman gathered her daughter into her arms.

"I think she's going to be okay," I said, shocked the woman was still conscious. "I have to go back for the others."

Knowing every minute counted, I hurried back to the ravine and climbed into the back seat of the car. I unbuckled the boy's seat belt. He stirred and groaned, his eyes fluttering open.

"Hi, I'm Hannah. I'm going to get you out of here. Where are you hurt?"

"My legs and my head."

The driver's seat was pushed up against him. We both had to work to free his pinned legs. Grunting and groaning, I eventually dragged him out.

Even though this was my second trip back up the ravine, the boy was much easier to carry. Because he was conscious, he wasn't the dead weight his sister had been. As he held on to my neck and buried his face in my hair, I learned his name was Timmy and his favorite thing was fire trucks.

When I put Timmy in the back seat of the SUV, I saw that his mom was struggling to remain conscious.

I faced a moment of indecision. The man might already be dead. It had been tough carrying the kids, and I had no idea how I was going to get a large man up the ravine. Besides, if I took the time to get him, it might be too late for the mom.

Hesitating, I realized it wasn't really a decision. I wouldn't be able to live with myself if I didn't at least try. Having a sudden epiphany, I opened the back of my SUV and removed a tow rope and a tarp.

Since I'd always had a healthy fear of just about every worst case scenario, I took seriously the motto, "Always be prepared." My phobias insured I had well-stocked emergency supplies. I'd just never imagined this situation was one I'd need to prepare for.

When I got to the sedan, I found the man's pulse still barely registering life. It was probably good he was unconscious. He was stuck. I pushed and pulled, trying not to think about any other pain or injuries I may be inflicting. I had to get him out.

He wasn't budging even a little. Panting and sweating, I tried to catch my breath. But it kept coming in short gasps.

I couldn't do it! Great sobs scraped past my throat. I was losing it!

"Please help me!" I prayed desperately, yelling at the top of my lungs.

I crawled over him, kicking and punching his seat like a madwoman.

To my shock, the seat broke. I quickly removed the seat back, using the space to pull the man from behind. His lifeless body finally slid from its cage.

Breathing heavily, I dragged him out of the car and onto the tarp I had positioned. I wrapped the tarp around him and tied one end of the rope under his arms. Grabbing the other end, I pulled. The tarp slid across the snow.

Even with the tarp, the man was dead weight. I'd heard that adrenaline had been known to give a person superhuman strength. That and some divine assistance is the only explanation I have for how my 5'6'' frame was able to drag that man uphill out of the ravine and then lift him into the rear of the SUV.

Finally back inside my SUV, my frozen fingers gripped

the steering wheel in terror as I drove through the snow. The woman was unconscious now. I had to get to the lodge.

Timmy was the only one conscious. He was amazingly calm. We talked about his Christmas list. From Hot Wheels to remote controls, Timmy wanted such variety of cars and trucks that Santa would have his work cut out for him.

My breath caught with relief as I saw the lights of Silver Springs through the swirling snow. Stopping in front of the lodge, I jumped out. Frantic, I yelled, banging my fists on the front door. An elderly man I didn't recognize opened it.

I don't remember what I told him. Everything I said seemed like gibberish in my head, but he apparently understood.

"Go get McAllister!" he called to an older woman near the stairs. He then turned and explained to me that a doctor was vacationing at the lodge.

The older man and two others gently carried each person to the large living room where the doctor known as McAllister was putting on a pair of rubber gloves.

Scanning the patients, he called to the man from the door. "George, we're going to need a helicopter."

My eyes met the doctor's blue-green ones and held. He was a lot younger than I had expected, with a strong face and dark, wavy blond hair to go with those rather incredible eyes.

"Who's injured the worst?" he asked.

"The man," I replied. "I'm not sure he's still alive. His pulse was very weak even before I pulled him out of the wreck."

Dr. McAllister's eyes shot back to me, sizing me up.

Obviously having questions, he said instead, "I need some help."

Maybe he assumed I had some medical training. Then again, maybe I was just the best choice of assistants. The other three guys in the room didn't look like they would be able to tell the difference between a pair of tweezers and a chainsaw.

I followed Dr. McAllister as he checked each patient. I don't remember what he did. I was in a daze, simply following his orders.

The loud chopping of a helicopter broke the hush of the room. Paramedics rushed in with gurneys and quickly transferred the family to the waiting helicopter. As the lights and sounds faded away, Dr. McAlister took my hand, led me to a couch in front of the fire, and placed a mug of hot cocoa in my stiff fingers.

He sat down beside me, his gaze concerned. "I haven't even asked if you are hurt."

"No. Just cold."

He wrapped a blanket around me, saying, "Can you tell me what happened?"

Almost like a recitation, I recounted every detail, but it was like I was talking about someone else. I felt nothing.

When I finished, I asked softly, "Are they going to be alright, Dr. McAlister?" I vaguely noticed that my hands around the mug had begun shaking.

He winced. Seeing my cocoa was about to slosh out of my hands, he took the mug, put it on the coffee table, and held my cold hands in his warm ones.

His eyes met mine. "Call me Seth. And I'm not really a

doctor, not yet anyway. I'm in medical school. George is an old friend who tends to exaggerate my accomplishments and ignore my faults."

"I'm Hannah."

Knowing I was still waiting for an answer, he sighed. "I think the kids are going to be fine. I'm not sure about the mom. She's lost a lot of blood. I don't think the dad will make it. They'll do everything possible, but his chances are very slim."

I appreciated his honesty. "I don't know why my hands are shaking," I murmured. Thinking back to what I had done, I felt a burning behind my eyes. "I had to do a lot of maneuvering to get the man out of the car. It was really rough. Maybe I hurt him more."

I whispered. "Do you think he'll die because of something I did?"

Warm tears rolled down my face. Seth took my face in his gentle hands, lifting my chin so our eyes met.

"Hannah, none of those people would have made it without you. Do you understand? They would have all died. You told me, but I still don't understand how you did it. I do know that you saved them." His thumb massaged my cheek. "I don't think I've ever met a woman who was so strong and brave."

I let out an almost hysterical giggle. "I'm not brave at all. If you only knew. My own shadow scares me regularly!"

"You did what had to be done even though you were afraid. I call that bravery."

Seeing his honest face looking at me with such admiration, I lost it. The shaking hands turned into full body convulsions. The hysterical giggling transformed into heaving sobs. I couldn't catch my breath. My throat, eyes, and chest burned, but I was so cold. I relived yet again every last detail of the night. But this time, I felt everything.

Seth held me close, caressing my hair, wiping my tears, whispering words of comfort. His lips traced gentle kisses across my forehead. While this would normally be a strange intimacy with someone I just met, with Seth it felt right. Comforting.

Eventually I felt the warmth of his strong arms seep through the cold. My sobs lessened as my body relaxed. I clung to Seth. I felt a blessed numbness as warmth stole over me. My eyelids grew impossibly heavy.

As if in a dream, I felt myself being carried, floating up the stairs until I was laid gently upon a soft bed. Seth covered me with a blanket. I tried to speak, but I couldn't remember any words. I felt a gentle kiss on my forehead and a whispered, "Good night." My last memory was of those blue-green eyes and a feather-light touch on my face.

CHAPTER TWO

WHEN I awoke in the morning, light was streaming through my bedroom window. I shot out of bed and almost passed out. My aching head spun wildly, making me sink back down on the bed. Gradually, the pain and dizziness lessened.

Hurriedly, I showered and dressed, thankful someone had brought in my suitcase.

I needed to find Abby. I needed to get an update on how the injured family was doing. But most of all, I needed to see Seth.

It hadn't occurred to me last night to ask for my sister. I was more than a little distracted, and I guess I had just assumed she had already gone to bed. It was just like my matchmaker sister to have a "prospect" around for my visit. Only this time, I would thank her.

Looking in the mirror, I nervously smoothed wayward

strands of auburn hair back with the rest of my ponytail. I needed some serious help for my hair. Maybe Abby could give me some pointers. Hopefully, the light of day wouldn't make Seth change his mind about me.

I found Abby in the kitchen.

"Now, Abby, I know you sleep like a log, but seriously, I don't understand how you could have slept through everything last night."

Abby squealed and met me for a hug. Though she was two years older than me, I was taller by a couple of inches. Abby was cute and petite. People had always said that we looked alike: same ocean-blue eyes, high cheekbones, and subtle dimples. However, I still thought that where looks were concerned, Abby swam on the better side of the gene pool.

Abby gently pushed me toward a chair and started piling food on a plate. I swear she always tried to get me to pack on the pounds when I visited.

"What happened last night, Hannah? I finally had to stop waiting and go to bed. I was so relieved when I peaked in your room this morning and saw you there."

"But Seth filled you in, right? How is the injured family? Are the parents still alive?"

Abby looked at me with confusion. "What are you talking about, Hannah? And who in the heck is Seth?"

"Come on, Abby, that isn't funny! I was Superwoman last night and rescued a family who'd had an accident in the snowstorm. A helicopter came to the lodge and took them to the hospital. No one told you about the helicopter?"

Abby stared at me like I'd lost my mind. "Hannah,

maybe you should sit down. Are you not feeling well?"

"I'm fine! But I want to know what's going on! Where's Seth? He'll explain it to you."

"Hannah, there isn't anyone here at Silver Springs named Seth. There was no injured family or a helicopter here last night. And…" She walked over and lifted the window blind to reveal a sunshiny day with only a moderate amount of snow. "We haven't had any new snow in at least two weeks!"

I stared out the window and shook my head. "That isn't possible."

Abby's husband, Tom, sauntered into the kitchen. After Abby explained the situation, he confirmed everything.

"Maybe you just had a very vivid dream," Abby suggested.

"No, Abby, it happened. I know it did."

But then I started to doubt. What if it hadn't happened?

"Here, Hannah," Abby said, sliding the plate of food closer, "Maybe you'll feel better after you've eaten some breakfast."

I obediently stuffed some food in my mouth, my mind jumping in a hundred different directions. I thought it had happened. It had all been so real.

"You've always had an overactive imagination, Hannah" Abby teased. "What did you eat last night?

"I don't remember," I mumbled absent-mindedly. I just couldn't wrap my mind around the fact that everything I had experienced last night, all the terror, the strength, the emotions, had been part of a dream.

Seth... could he really have been a figment of my imagination?

Feeling completely lost, I looked down, trying to blink back the sudden moisture in my eyes. My gaze focused on angry red marks marring my right wrist. Scratches!

Suddenly shaky, I got to my feet. "It was real, Abby. Everything was real! A family went off the road into a ravine and hit a tree. I saved them. Me, wimpy, me!"

Holding up my arm as evidence, I continued. "I got these scratches from a branch last night as I was sliding down the embankment to rescue them."

Seeing the doubts and concern still in Abby's eyes, I pressed on. "It happened, Abby! I know it did! I brought them here to Silver Springs. A medical student named Seth McAllister treated them. He cared about me and thought I was brave. I remember everything, for Pete's sake! He had gorgeous blue-green eyes and a tiny triangle scar on his right cheekbone. Crazy or not, Abby, I just can't let this go."

Tom's forehead wrinkled. "I remember someone mentioning an accident like that. Remember Abby, when we bought the place? Several people warned us that the road could be dangerous in the winter. They mentioned an accident."

"I remember. But that accident was at least five years ago."

"That sounds like the same story a gas station attendant told me yesterday," I remembered. "He said everyone in that accident had died."

Neither Tom nor Abby could recall any other details.

"I'm sorry, Abby. I have to leave. I need to find out what

happened to me yesterday. I have to know."

Despite my sister's protests, I was in my SUV ten minutes later and headed back down the mountain. All my fears, let alone my vivid memories, seemed almost silly in the bright sunshine and clear roads.

When I got to the town of Sonora, I located the public library. Thankfully, they had old copies of the local paper on microfilm.

Using the information I had been given, I searched for an accident that had occurred about five years ago.

I found it. Goosebumps covered every inch of my skin. I couldn't breathe.

The date on the newspaper was exactly five years ago today. That meant the accident had been five years ago yesterday. The title of the article was: "Mystery Woman Saves Accident Victims." I read the article rapidly, then went back and reread it. It told how an unknown woman had rescued the Lawson family when their car had slid into a ravine and hit a tree on the road to Silver Springs. After getting all four victims out of the mangled car and into her own SUV, she took them to Silver Springs Lodge where a medical student named Seth McAlister treated them until a rescue helicopter arrived. The next morning, the mystery woman was gone. Her SUV, her suitcase, every trace was gone. Despite serious injuries, the children were expected to make full recoveries, but the parents were still listed in critical condition.

I anxiously searched the newspapers for the following days, reading updates and background information about the family as well as the search for the woman. In an article a week later, it was reported that both parents had survived and were being upgraded to stable condition.

The final article I found featured Seth McAlister. He had been interviewed about the mystery woman, saying she deserved to be recognized for her courageous rescue. He was concerned about her sudden disappearance and was offering a sizeable reward for any information leading to her whereabouts. The only clue to her identity was her first name: Hannah.

By the time I finished reading, my mind was in chaos. I had apparently just experienced the impossible!

Finding a computer station, I logged onto the Internet. I typed in 'Seth McAlister' and stopped. Going back, I inserted 'Dr.' in front of his name, figuring he had undoubtedly finished medical school in the past five years. It took a few minutes to find that his current place of employment was the University of California San Francisco Medical Center.

Not stopping to think, I grabbed my purse, ignored the curious stare of the librarian, and got back in my car. After three hours and several arguments with my GPS, I finally pulled into a parking garage near the hospital. It was nearing 5:00 in the evening.

The hospital was huge. I had no idea where Seth worked or even if he was on shift. If I did manage to find him, he may not remember me. Who was I kidding? I had no idea if this Seth McAlister was even the one from the newspaper articles.

Palms sweating and heart thumping, I chose the largest building and went straight to the information desk. Three elderly ladies carefully punched keys on a computer, finally directing me to the fourth floor.

The nurse at the station there looked me up and down with frosty blue eyes.

"Dr. McAlister has left for the evening. I could give you his office number if you wanted to leave a message. As I'm sure you're aware, he is extremely busy."

I got the strange impression that I was being reprimanded for asking for the doctor in the first place. Not having a choice, I went back down to the lobby.

What should I do now? As uncharacteristic as it was, I hadn't made a plan. Maybe tomorrow I could look up the family I had saved — the Lawsons. Maybe I really was crazy and neither Seth nor the Lawsons would actually know me. But, I had come this far; I had to at least try.

Before reaching the front door of the hospital, I was overwhelmed by a wave of sheer exhaustion. I stopped and took out my cell phone. I could probably save time by calling hotels to check for vacancies.

Turning and scanning the room for a couch, I saw a man round the corner and head for the front doors. Seth. My tongue was suddenly tied, my feet unable to move.

Five feet away, he glanced up. Instant recognition and shock flooded his handsome face. He stopped, staring at me.

"Hannah," he choked out in a strangled voice.

My eyes met his blue-green. "Seth," I whispered.

Before I could collect my thoughts and form an explanation, Seth crossed the distance and enfolded me in his arms. For a long moment he just held me, as if afraid I would disappear.

Finally drawing back, he studied me.

"Hannah, I can't believe it's really you. You're exactly

the same. Where have you been? It's been five years! I've tried everything to find you."

As I stood looking into Seth's handsome face and feeling his arms around me, all the confusion and uncertainty faded. My world finally felt right.

I smiled into those beautiful blue-green eyes and laughed lightly. "Would you believe me if I told you that to me it was only yesterday?"

Seth looked confused, but then his eyes traced the contours of my face and he murmured, "It's been so long, Hannah, so long." His gaze focused on my lips. I knew he was going to kiss me. I leaned forward.

"Seth?"

At the sound of his name, Seth jerked. A guilty, pained expression crossed his face. He quickly smoothed his features and turned with a smile to the approaching woman. She was the same rude nurse I had encountered upstairs.

"Seth," she repeated, "who's this?"

"Katherine," he replied, "I'd like you to meet Hannah. Remember? This is the girl who saved the Lawson family five years ago."

Turning to me, pain again flitted through Seth's expression. "Hannah, this is Katherine Colson,... my fiancé."

CHAPTER THREE

HIS *fiancé?* As waves of shock rolled over me, I still managed to plaster a smile on my face and stick my hand out to greet Katherine.

Even in her "Hello, Kitty" nursing scrubs, Katherine Colson was exquisite. She was tall and modelesque with her platinum blond hair pulled back to reveal high cheekbones and what looked to be real diamond earrings. Who wore diamond earrings with scrubs? As Katherine reluctantly shook my hand with her frosty, manicured one, I realized the answer to my own question. A woman who wore diamonds with scrubs was one who wanted all other women to feel exactly how I felt right now — inferior in every way.

"Hannah?" Katherine questioned. Then, with a friendly smile and a tone that contrasted the icy glare in her eyes, she asked, "Seth, is this the Hannah who disappeared? The Hannah you just about went insane trying to find?"

Not knowing how to reply, I said simply, "It's nice to

meet you."

"You have no idea how *nice* it is to finally meet *you*! I had begun to think that everyone had a Hannah hallucination five years ago triggered by a bizarre astrological event or maybe just a massive amount of paint fumes. You have no idea how relieved I am to know you actually exist!"

Katherine's words and sweet, complimentary tone were fake. I didn't know if it was a veneer for Seth's benefit or if it was just the way Katherine was. By the look in her eyes, I did know she absolutely hated me. If looks could kill, I would have been brutally murdered the instant she knew my name, and my ashes would have already been scattered around the four corners of the world.

Katherine turned to Seth, "And you never mentioned that Hannah was so young! I had the impression she'd been about your age five years ago. But, I see now that she had to have been a teenager! That just makes her bravery all the more remarkable."

Obviously highly uncomfortable with Katherine's interest in me, Seth replied quietly, "She looks the same."

"I'm older than I look," I defended, feeling very young, immature, and homely compared to the beautiful, well-spoken creature before me. But, obviously, that is exactly the way Katherine wanted me to feel.

"Well, Hannah, I'm dying to have this mystery finally solved," Katherine said. "Why did you disappear five years ago? Where have you been?"

I gripped the keys in my hand tighter. I was definitely not going to spill my guts in front of Katherine. "Um... it's kind of complicated."

Realizing I really had nothing to lose, I decided to be

direct and honest. I turned to Set, saying, "I was hoping we could go somewhere so we could talk and I could explain some things."

Before Seth could answer, Katherine slipped her arm around his waist and answered for him. "Oh, I'm sorry, Hannah! We just can't right now. Seth and I have an appointment this evening with the caterer for our wedding. In fact, we'd better be leaving or we'll be late."

With tortured eyes, Seth looked at me. "Hannah, could you give us a minute? I need to talk to Katherine."

"Sure." I walked a few feet away and pretended to be fascinated with a framed quilt on display. I didn't intentionally eavesdrop. Okay, maybe I did. But I only caught snippets of their rather heated conversation:

"Absolutely not, Seth…. We've had this appointment for months!"

"I need to talk to her… I need closure on this."

Katherine was visibly angry and lashed out a whispered tirade I couldn't understand.

Nodding in what appeared to be acceptance, I heard Seth ask, "How long…?"

After more whispered murmurings, I heard Katherine sigh dramatically. She then stood on her tiptoes and kissed Seth possessively, probably for my benefit. Then, shooting me a pointed look of warning, she squeezed Seth's hand one more time and glided out of the hospital.

Seth walked toward me, his hand at the back of his neck, probably trying to loosen some of the tension there.

"I'm sorry, Hannah, but would you be able to meet me in about two hours?" His eyes looked tormented as they seemed to beg me to understand. "I really have to go to this appointment."

"Sure, just tell me where. I'll go check in to my hotel." We started walking toward the hospital doors.

"Where are you staying?" He asked.

I blushed. "Well, I haven't exactly had a chance to book a room yet. Can you recommend a decent hotel nearby that doesn't cost an arm and a leg?"

Seth gave me directions to a hotel a couple blocks from the hospital. "We could meet at the diner across the street from there," he said.

"Okay. I guess I'll see you in a couple of hours." I clutched my keys and turned to walk to my car.

"Hannah," Seth's voice stopped me. "Ruby's Diner in two hours, right?"

Turning back around, I saw the expression of an insecure little boy on his face.

"You'll meet me?" he asked. "You won't disappear again?"

"I'll be there. I promise."

"Hannah, what's your last name?" Seth asked.

"Kraeger. Hannah Kraeger."

"And how do you spell that?"

I laughed. Then, very slowly and concisely, I spelled my last name.

Seth nodded, remaining serious.

"Do you want my birth certificate and social security number as well?" I asked innocently.

A slow smile spread across Seth's face, easing some of the tension.

"Actually, I think your license and registration will probably be enough," he replied.

My laughter died away in distraction. All thoughts of a witty retort fled, and I stood like a gawking teenager, mesmerized by the way laughter danced across Seth's eyes. As his blue-green eyes locked with my own, I felt electricity sparking the few feet between us. Still transfixed, I watched as the dancing lights in his eyes slowly faded. He cleared his throat and deliberately broke eye contact with me.

"I'd better get going," he said.

"I'll see you later," I replied, trying to ignore my embarrassment and muster up as much false cheer as possible. Waving, I turned and quickly fled to the parking garage. Sliding into my SUV, I made a mental note to avoid eye contact with Seth at all cost from now on. It wasn't worth the pain.

TWO hours later, I was sitting in a red vinyl booth when Seth walked into the diner, his hair windblown and his expression a bit frantic. When he saw my wave, the most incredible smile broke across his face. Brilliant white teeth flashed, revealing deep dimples in a chiseled face that bore a hint of a five o'clock shadow. It was the kind of smile that made women swoon, and it was directed at me.

In my peripheral vision, I thought I saw at least two women fall over from just the reflected radiance of that smile as he walked toward me. I don't know for sure though, because, despite my best intentions, my eyes were already locked with a pair of blue-green eyes sparkling with pure joy.

"You're here," he breathed as he slid onto the vinyl across from me. "After everything with Katherine..." He paused, appearing to rethink what he was saying, then finished simply, "I was afraid you wouldn't come."

"I promised." I answered, shrugging my shoulders. Part of me wanted to ask about Katherine, wanted to know all the details of their relationship and how he felt about her. Part of me wanted to ask how he could look at me the way he did if he really loved another woman. But I didn't ask. The greater part of me didn't want to risk the hurt of knowing.

The waitress came and took our orders. Wasting no time, Seth jumped in with questions.

"So, Hannah Kraeger, what happened five years ago?"

I wasn't even sure how to explain things. I was nervous that he wouldn't believe me and would think I was crazy. But, Seth wasn't mine to lose. I figured I might as well tell him everything. I couldn't be much worse off even if he did think I was crazy.

I took two sheets of paper out of my purse and unfolded them on the table in front of him.

"These are copies of my driver's license and car title," I explained with a slight smile.

Seth smiled back, "Thanks! It'll be much easier to find you with this information. But, as much as I appreciate this insurance against any future disappearance, I don't see what this has to do with what happened five years ago."

"Look at the dates," I said softly. "My birthdate. The date I came in possession of the vehicle. I'm twenty-three now. Obviously, I did not look eighteen when you saw me last. You said yourself that I looked exactly the same then as I do now. My SUV, the same one I drove the family to the lodge *five* years ago, wasn't even mine until a year later when my dad bought it for me.

"I don't understand." Seth's forehead was crinkled in confusion. "How is this possible?"

"I don't know how or why, but what happened five years ago for you, happened yesterday for me."

Seth stared at me a long moment before saying slowly, "Maybe you'd better start at the beginning."

So I did. I started when I was heading up the mountain to my sister's lodge. I told him everything, even repeating the parts I'd already told him yesterday / five years ago about saving the Lawson family. I told him how I remembered talking to him on the couch by the fire. How I started crying and he comforted me. How I remembered him carrying me upstairs and laying me on a bed. How he kissed me on the forehead before whispering, "Good night."

I then explained how I woke up this morning and found my sister and her husband had no memory of last night's events. How I felt like I'd gone crazy when I saw that there obviously hadn't even been a snowstorm. How I went to the library and found information on the accident that had apparently been five years ago. How I looked up Dr. Seth McAlister on the Internet and drove to the hospital hoping to find him. How I didn't even know if he was the right Seth

McAlister since he'd only been a med student *yesterday*.

"And now we're here. And I have no idea what happened, let alone how or why."

Saying that Seth seemed shocked would be a vast understatement. He didn't say anything for several minutes. Our food arrived and I completely ignored it, not having an appetite until I knew Seth's reaction.

Instead, I grabbed a pen left on the side of the table for signing receipts and began doodling on my paper napkin. Doodling was a nervous habit of mine. Of course, I doodled when I wasn't nervous too: to concentrate, out of boredom, or for fun. I just liked to doodle.

"I believe you." My pen jerked at Seth's soft words. "Under normal circumstances, I wouldn't. I would probably recommend a good psychologist and some heavy-duty anti-psychotic drugs." Gently, he slid the pen out of my grasp, forcing me to stop doodling and look up into his smiling eyes. "But, unfortunately, in this case, I would have to recommend the same treatment for myself, because five years ago *I saw you.*"

"You weren't eighteen," he continued. "You looked exactly the same. Same face. Same hair style. Even the same..." He gently took my right hand in his own. My hand tingled with his touch, sending goosebumps up my arm. Turning my hand over, he carefully traced the skin on my inner wrist. ". . . cuts on your right wrist you must have gotten somehow during the rescue. I saw these same cuts five years ago or last night, depending on your perspective."

"Thank you," I whispered, relishing the sensation of his hand holding mine. As if remembering Katherine, he suddenly closed his eyes and, seemingly reluctantly, released my hand.

As Seth began eating his burger, I finally dared to look at my own plate and realized how ravenous I was. My club sandwich and fries looked heavenly.

"That being said," Seth continued, his brow creased in thought as he ate, "I don't understand it. Has anything even remotely like this ever happened to you before?"

"No, nothing. No history of mental health problems either. In fact, I've always had remarkably good health."

"What about the rest of your family? Any history of extraordinary experiences?"

"No, not at all. I already told you about my older sister, Abby. She was about ready to have me committed when I told her what had happened. My dad raised two daughters by himself, and he is still remarkably sane. In fact, he is about as normal and practical as you can get. My mom died in childbirth with me, but I've certainly never heard of anything unusual happening in her life."

I appreciated that Seth didn't offer any meaningless platitudes like most other people about the death of my mom. His eyes flashed sympathy, but he wasn't sidetracked.

"How did you feel when you woke up this morning?"

I thought back. "I was dizzy and had a really intense headache, but that didn't last for long. My memories of last night were clear, and, like I said, I fully expected to find you at the lodge."

Seth sighed, his frustration apparent. "The scientist in

me would like an explanation."

"I feel the same way," I replied, "but the only explanation I can come up with is based more on faith than on science. For some reason, God used me to save that family. He's God. I guess he's allowed to break his own rules of science to accomplish his purpose."

"I'm a man of faith, too," Seth replied. "But I do have to admit that my faith does need a little stretching if it's going to include time travel."

We ate in silence for a few minutes, each lost in thought. Despite the appearance, the club sandwich was mediocre; it could have been improved with more bacon. The fries were especially good though, salty and crunchy the way I like them.

Finishing his meal first, Seth was the one to break the silence. "You're right, though, Hannah, the Lawson family would have all died if it wasn't for you."

"How are they doing? Have you kept in contact with them? I saw in the newspaper articles that everyone had survived and were recovering."

"Last time I talked to them, they were all doing great. Everything about your rescue and their recovery has been miraculous. Neither the mom or the dad, Kelly and Matt, were expected to live when they arrived at the hospital. Now the whole family is healthy and happy. Matt has a slight stutter when he's tired and a little lingering stiffness, but that's it. I know they would love to see you, Hannah."

"I would like to see them. Maybe it would help me to come to terms with all that has happened."

"They live about an hour away. I could call and arrange a meeting; maybe even for tomorrow, if you'd like."

I was suddenly unsure, my trademark insecurities revealing themselves. "I don't suppose you could... I mean I'm sure they won't recognize me. It was really dark, and everyone but Timmy was unconscious. Do you think you might... ? I mean, is there any way you could... come with me?" Studying my napkin doodles and refusing to make eye contact with Seth, I realized I was probably acting and sounding like an immature child.

"Never mind," I suddenly backpedaled. "I can go myself. I'm sure you're busy, and Katherine probably wouldn't appreciate..."

"Hannah," Seth interrupted. "I would love to go with you."

I waited for the "but." It never came.

"Both the Lawson's and I looked for you," he explained. "I know that Matt and Kelly felt cheated that they hadn't been given the opportunity to thank you. I would absolutely love to be there with you when they finally get that chance."

My eyes were tearing, and I could only manage to nod.

"I don't have to work until tomorrow evening, so I'll call the Lawsons in the morning and then call you."

I wrote my cell number on the back of the copy of my driver's license. Stifling a yawn, I realized how tired I was.

"I really need to get to bed," I explained, trying to mask another yawn. "It's been a really long twenty-four hours for me."

"Of course," Seth agreed, hurriedly paying for the entire dinner bill despite my protest. "I'll walk you across the street to your hotel."

Exiting the restaurant, our footsteps echoed a lonely sound against the pavement.

Thinking about tomorrow, I asked, "Do you see the Lawsons very often?"

"I try to keep in contact. Matt Lawson has become a good friend of mine. Besides, until now, they've kind of been my only connection to you — the proof that you existed."

I stuffed my freezing hands into my coat pockets and tried to ignore the desire to walk closer to Seth.

"You said that they tried to find me, too?"

"Yes, but eventually they gave up. We couldn't find a single lead. Now, they like to think of you as their guardian angel."

I laughed, then continued with mock indignation, "What, you weren't content with the angel explanation, Seth?"

"No, I wasn't. Remember, I'd witnessed your all-too-human reaction to an extremely stressful experience."

I grimaced. "You're right. That meltdown wasn't exactly angelic. Thank you for being there, by the way."

Remembering the closeness of that night and the way Seth had held me, I felt as if the air between us suddenly became charged. Not trusting myself to not reach for him, I quickened my step and tried to lighten the mood.

"One thing I don't understand. Why me? If God needed someone to go back in time to save the Lawsons, I would've thought he would have sent a 250 pound linebacker who moonlights as a paramedic, not — "

"130 pound Hannah?" Seth finished for me with an ornery grin.

"How did you…?"

"Driver's license, remember?" Seth held up the copy still in his hand.

Now at the door to the hotel, I turned to Seth, knowing my cheeks were turning an embarrassing shade I could only term magenta.

"Seriously, though, Hannah. It seems to me that God sent the most capable person he could have. You did it. I still don't know how, but you saved the entire family. No linebacker paramedic could have done better."

"Thank you, Seth."

Meeting his eyes, I saw a flash of insecurity in their blue-green depths. "You'll be here tomorrow, right Hannah? You won't disappear on me again?"

Trying to make light, I answered. "Well, you have all my information just in case. But, I'll be here, barring Super Hannah doesn't get any new time traveling missions from God, that is."

Seth didn't seem to appreciate my humor.

"I'm not ready to joke about it yet, Hannah." His eyes locked with mine and my breath quickened. "Five years ago, I knew you weren't a figment of my imagination, that you weren't an angel. But your tears weren't the only reason I knew. I talked to you, comforted you, touched you. Everything in me said you were real. I couldn't handle it if you disappeared again."

He raised his hand as if to touch my cheek, but then let it drop to his side and looked away. "I guess we can talk more tomorrow. Sleep well, Hannah." Turning, he disappeared past the halo of the street lights.

CHAPTER FOUR

BUT we didn't really talk on the way to see the Lawsons; at least we didn't talk about anything important. Instead, we filled time with small talk.

Neither of us even mentioned Katherine. It was like we couldn't bring ourselves to mention the pink elephant riding in the car with us. For my part, I wanted to forget Katherine. For just a few hours, I wanted to have Seth to myself, even if his friendship was all I could ever have.

Seth drove a silver BMW convertible. While impressed with the luxury, I imagined it would slide like a goldfish on ice in the snow. My SUV didn't have the seat warmers and all the bells and whistles that Seth's car did, but I'd take safety over comfort any day. Sure, Seth lived in the San Francisco Bay Area and would probably need snow tires about as often as you'd need a yacht in Kansas, but, just in case, I was ready. Thankfully, we weren't headed back up the Sierras, and the worst we had to deal with was traffic.

Seth seemed a good driver, and I managed not to freak out too much about letting someone else drive. I was typically uncomfortable with my own driving, but someone else's driving would usually put me on the verge of a panic attack. Luckily, our small talk seemed to distract my white knuckles from their usual grip on the seat.

I asked about Seth's work. Reading between the lines, I gathered that Dr. Seth McAllister, though just beginning his career, was already a highly respected physician. He specialized in treating difficult cases, and some of his research had led to progress and success in cases that had been considered hopeless.

"So, you're an Art Major at the California State University in Sacramento," Seth said, taking his turn at our own version of Twenty Questions. "Isn't there a big art school in San Francisco? What made you choose CSUS instead?"

"I got a scholarship for Chemistry at CSUS. They let me use the scholarship if I did a Chemistry Minor. I also work for the Chemistry department, helping with research documentation. Besides that, I wanted to stay close to my dad. He still lives in Jackson, where I grew up. Sacramento is close enough that I can spend my weekends with him and make sure he's taking care of himself."

"A Major in Art and a Minor in Chemistry is an unusual combination," Seth commented.

"Everyone says that," I admitted. "I've always been good at Science, especially Chemistry. It comes easy to me. My Chemistry professors are still unhappy with me because

I didn't choose one of the sciences as my major. I love Art, though. Strangely, it both challenges and relaxes me. It's what makes me happy, my default activity. It's what I do when I have nothing to do."

"So you graduate in May, right? What are you planning to do after graduation?"

"I wish I knew. I should have graduated a while ago, but when I initially started college, I had about 4 different majors. I could decide what to do. Art finally won out, but it isn't necessarily the smartest choice for someone who enjoys food as much as I do. I really don't have the temperament to be a starving artist. I guess my dream would be to own an art gallery that featured the work of great artists, including my own, of course." I added with mock pride.

"Judging by your napkin doodles last night, I would say you are a very good artist."

"Thanks! I'll be sure to make a nice display of my doodled napkins in my exclusive art gallery."

We took an exit off the freeway and started making our way through the town of Danville.

I continued, "Maybe I should stick to Plan B, though. I've thought about getting certified to be an Art teacher. I like kids, and, while I'll never get rich, it may be rewarding to teach something I love."

We made a couple of turns until we were driving through tree-lined residential streets heavily bedecked for Christmas. I knew we were getting close.

"Seth, the Lawsons know I'm coming with you, right?"

Seth looked a little sheepish. "No, I just said I was bringing someone for them to meet. I figured it would be better to show them Hannah in person."

As we pulled to the curb in front of a modest, one-story brown house with nice landscaping, I had a sudden thought. "What are we going to tell them about where I've been for the past five years?"

"I figured we'd tell them the truth. I know the truth doesn't seem to make sense, but no other explanation would make sense either. Who knows, maybe they'll actually believe it. Remember, these are the same people who thought you were an angel."

"I guess you're right," I replied as we got out of the car.

Normally, I would have been extremely nervous about going into this situation. Sweaty palms and heart palpitations were my usual reactions to unfamiliar or stressful circumstances, but, with Seth walking beside me to the front door, I didn't feel my normal nerves. It would have felt even better if Seth would have held my hand, but he didn't touch me. I knew he wouldn't.

The door opened when Seth knocked. As we entered the living room, I recognized Kelly and Matt. They looked wonderful, like superhero versions of the shadows I had seen two days ago. Their daughter, Maddie, now looked to be about thirteen and, typical for her age, was sitting on the couch glued to the TV.

Timmy, who would be about ten now, rounded the corner from the kitchen area. Locking eyes with him, I saw shock wash over his face, followed by a slow smile.

"Hi, Hannah!" he said, almost nonchalantly.

"Hannah?" Matt and Kelly repeated, looking from me to Seth and back to me. "Seth, is this Hannah? *Our* Hannah?"

Seth grinned widely. "Matt and Kelly Lawson, I'd like you to meet Hannah Kraeger. Yes, she is *our* Hannah. The same Hannah who pulled you out of the wreck and saved your lives five years ago."

Kelly squealed and threw her arms around me and then Seth. Matt followed close behind with his own bear hug. Maddie turned off the tv and shyly hugged me as well.

Finally, I turned to Timmy. "You recognized me, Timmy?" I asked.

"Sure," he said with a shrug. "I remember that night you saved us pretty good. Besides, you look the same." Stopping, Timmy looked me over from head to toe before continuing in a slightly disappointed voice. "I guess this means that you aren't really an angel."

Everyone laughed and the emotional atmosphere lifted a little.

"No, Timmy, I can very safely say, and my older sister would confirm, that I am definitely not an angel."

Seeing that he was still a bit disappointed with my non-celestial background, I continued, "This non-angel does have an early Christmas present for you though, Timmy. Or do you go by just Tim now?" At his nod, I reached into my oversized purse, trying to locate the item I had purchased at a drugstore that morning before Seth picked me up.

"Here it is!" I announced, plopping a miniature remote control car in Tim's outstretched hand. "I figured a kid your age could probably still appreciate a remote control car, especially a miniature one that does flips and twists like this one."

"Cool! Thanks!" Tim excitedly ran to the kitchen to charge his new gift and try it out.

At Seth's inquiring look, I explained, "When we were driving to the lodge after the accident, Tim told me all about his Christmas list. The kid is crazy about toy cars and trucks, or at least he was five years ago."

"He still is," Maddie grumbled with a roll of her eyes.

"Oh, Maddie, I also have something for you." I fished around in my purse again. "I wasn't sure what you liked, so I just got you some of my favorite lip gloss to try."

Maddie's eyes lit up at the present. "Thanks! Let me go see how it looks."

As she ran to her room, I caught Seth trying to hide a grin.

"What?" I asked. "I couldn't get a present for one and not the other."

Turning my attention back to Matt and Kelly, I saw that they were both studying me closely with tears in their eyes.

"*Thank you* seems a poor way to express what you did for us that night," Matt said, his voice rough. "We all would have died if you had not been there and done what you did."

Uncomfortable with their thanks and praise, I replied. "*You're welcome* also seems inadequate. I'm just glad I was able to help and things have turned out so well for your family."

"Please, sit down, you two," Kelly said, gesturing to the couch. Kelly didn't seem to have any visible effects from the accident. In fact, she had the kind of looks I had always wanted. She was tall with curly short blond hair and a great figure.

"It was so sweet of you to bring gifts for Tim and Maddie," Kelly continued. "You must have an amazing memory to remember what was on a little boy's list five years ago."

"Well, it wasn't quite five years ago for Hannah," Seth inserted with a grin.

"I don't understand." Kelly said, both she and her husband looking confused. "I know my memory of that night is very fuzzy in parts, but the accident was five years ago day before yesterday."

"I would love to hear Hannah's version of what happened that night." Matt inserted.

Kelly nodded. "One thing I've never been able to figure out is how you managed to get Matt out of the car and up the ravine. He's a big guy. I don't think I could've done it, and I'm bigger than you. The wreckers who towed the car also couldn't figure out how we survived the accident, let alone how a young woman could have rescued all of us, especially Matt."

Looking at Matt now, I myself had no idea how I had managed to pull him out of that car. There was no other way to say it, Matt was huge. He was at least 6'2'' with broad shoulders and a heavily muscled frame. His size along with his dark hair and five o'clock shadow might have made him an imposing figure, but his expression was gentle and his smile sincere.

"I'd also like to know how and why you've managed to hide for the past five years," Matt said, his expression curious.

Seeing Seth nod encouragingly at me, I took a deep breath and once again retold the events as I knew them. Seth showed them the copies of my driver's license and car title.

"So you see," I concluded, "I don't know how, but apparently I traveled back in time to help your family five years ago. But, for me, that was just two days ago."

"Seth, you believe all of this?" Matt asked, his voice shaky.

Seth nodded. "There's really no other explanation. Besides, is it really more difficult to believe that Hannah was an angel sent to rescue you or a normal person sent back in time to rescue you?"

Matt and Kelly looked at each other, but before they could respond, a baby's cry sounded from down the hall.

Kelly stood. "I'll go get the baby. It sounds like nap time is over."

"The baby?" I asked, shocked. "Seth, you didn't tell me they had another baby."

"I guess it slipped my mind," Seth shrugged with a smile.

Kelly brought back a beautiful baby girl who looked to be about eight months old. "Hannah, I'd like to introduce you to the newest member of our family. This is Karis."

With her strawberry blond hair and blueberry eyes, the

baby was adorable. "Karis," I cooed to her, "what a pretty name for such a pretty baby."

"Karis is the Greek word for 'grace,'" Kelly explained. "We thought it appropriate considering Karis wouldn't even be here if it hadn't been for you and the grace of God. Her full name is Karis Hannah Lawson."

"I'm honored," I replied, tears burning my eyes. "May I hold her a minute?"

"Sure, you can try. She's kind of been going through the stranger anxiety phase, though, so don't be surprised if she pitches a fit."

Kelly handed me the baby, and I cuddled her close. Karis looked up to my face mere inches from her own and smiled.

Seeing the grin on her daughter's face, Kelly shook her head. "Sure, Karis, make a liar out of Mommy. What stranger anxiety?"

With my eyes locked with Karis's, the baby reached her chubby little hand up to touch my face. Suddenly, she grabbed my nose, hard.

"Ouch!" I yelped. "That hurts!"

Carefully, I extracted the little fingers embedded in my nose, and handed her back to Kelly. Eyes stinging from the pain, I rubbed my injury, already feeling it turn Rudolph red.

"Why did you have to do that, Karis?" I asked playfully. "Here I thought we had a Moment going, and you decide to take some souvenirs!"

Seth, Matt, and Kelly were all trying, unsuccessfully, to

control their laughter. Hearing the laughter, Karis started giggling too, and it was several minutes before any of them could look at me with a straight face.

Finally, Kelly announced. "Well, if you guys can pick yourself up from rolling on the floor, I'll have you watch this little monster while I get everyone some lunch."

"Before you do that, Kelly," I interrupted. "I really need to know. Do you believe my story?"

Matt shared a long look with Kelly before answering, "Yes, we do. I don't know how or why, but, given the evidence, I believe what you said is true. That just makes what happened to my family seem even more humbling and miraculous to me, though. God sure went to an awful lot of effort to save us. He must have some great plan for our lives."

Kelly nodded and opened her mouth to say something, but was interrupted by Tim, who stuck his head around the corner of the counter where he was playing with his car.

"Time traveling is even more awesome than being an angel, Hannah!" He quipped. "Do you think you'll get to go again sometime?"

Startled that the boy had been listening and caught every word of my story, it took me a few seconds to respond. "I certainly hope not, Tim. I'm glad I was able to help your family, but it was not an experience I'd want to repeat."

"Me either," I heard Seth say quietly, almost under his breath.

Tim joined Matt and Seth in front of the TV watching a football game, while I helped Kelly prepare a lunch of sandwiches, salad, and fruit.

While I cut vegetables for the salad, Kelly kept up the conversation.

"I'm so glad you finally showed up in our lives, especially for Seth's sake," she said in a voice that wouldn't be heard by anyone in the living room over the sounds of the TV and Karis's babbling.

"Why do you say that?" I asked.

"I think for us, it gives a little closure to be able to meet and thank the person who saved our lives. For Seth, I'm hoping that he'll also feel a sense of closure. It really messed him up when you disappeared."

"I heard that he looked for me but couldn't find any leads."

"We all looked for you, but Seth was almost obsessed. He personally interviewed everyone who had been at the lodge that day. He tried to file a missing person's report with the police department. He even hired private detectives"

"I'm not sure I understand why he was so determined to find me. We probably spent less than three hours together that night. Your family was able to come to terms with my disappearance and move on. Why wasn't Seth?"

Looking at me closely with raised eyebrows, Kelly said, "I think you probably already know the answer to that, Hannah. Judging by the way you look at him, I'd say the feeling was mutual. "

I felt my cheeks warm as Kelly continued. "I've never really believed in love at first sight, but I've never seen a man as torn up emotionally as Seth was about you. He told

Matt once that he'd never felt a connection with someone like the one he'd felt with you, never even knew such a thing could exist. He wasn't willing to give up on it. At one point, he even had a sketch artist do a picture of you, and then he hung the posters everywhere. He was right, by the way, the picture didn't do you justice."

"Well, obviously, he was eventually able to move on. How did that happen?"

"Seth and Matt have become good friends. Matt has his degree in counseling, and they spent a lot of time talking. After about two years of looking for you, Seth was in bad shape. He was discouraged, depressed, and was even considering dropping out of his final year of medical school. I don't really know what finally changed for him. I don't know if something Matt said finally got through or if he just came to the end of his rope, but he gave up on you and finally began living again.

"He seems to be fully recovered now. I mean, he's moved on with his life and is engaged to Katherine. I guess he was able to put to rest those romantic feelings for me."

"Have you two talked at all?" Kelly questioned with apparent exasperation. "Seth and Katherine have a lot of history together."

Seeing the question form on my lips, Kelly raised her hand to stop me. "Seth will have to tell you about that. I will tell you, though, that you two need to talk, for both your sakes. It's obvious by your faces that both of you are bottling up a lot of emotion and pain. If Seth is going to have a successful marriage with Katherine, he needs some closure."

Seeing me flinch at the phrase "marriage to Katherine," Kelly looked at me knowingly. "And, if you're going to be able to move on with your life when you obviously have strong feelings for a soon-to-be-married man, then you need to talk."

"Soon?" I repeated, startled. "How soon are they getting married?"

Ignoring my question, Kelly announced loudly, "Lunch is ready!"

Walking past me with a plate of sandwiches in her hands, she whispered fiercely, "Talk to him!"

Finding a seat at the table, my churning thoughts were interrupted when Maddie came sashaying into the room for lunch. My jaw fell open as I saw that the new lip gloss had been paired with an entire palette of heavy makeup. Beneath a liberal dusting of body glitter, Maddie's heavy blush and eyeliner were insignificant compared to the blue and purple eyeshadow caked above her eyes. To finish the look, Maddie's hair was swept into a dramatic up-do that was, judging by the aroma, held in place with about a gallon of hairspray.

Shutting my open mouth with a snap, I said honestly. "I like the lip gloss on you, Maddie. It looks very… natural." I refrained from adding that it was the only thing that looked natural.

"Thanks, Hannah!" Maddie beamed. "I like it too."

Matt and Seth were clearing their throats roughly while Kelly held a napkin to her mouth, literally trying to hold the laughter in. Finally catching Kelly's eye over Maddie's head, I mouthed the words, "I'm so sorry!"

At my words, Kelly lost control and tried to disguise great peals of laughter by coughing into her napkin.

"Are you okay, Mom?" Maddie asked.

"Just fine, Honey." Taking a deep cleansing breath, she urged, "Let's eat!"

Though we managed a relatively normal conversation through lunch, we did so without any eye contact. We all knew instinctively that if any of us looked at each other, we would revert to hysterical laughter that would embarrass poor Maddie.

After lunch, Seth and I thanked the Lawsons and said our goodbyes. I managed to kiss Karis's chubby cheeks without a repeat injury. Tim and Maddie both hugged me goodbye. The entire family thanked me profusely again and said that they would love to have me become a regular part of their lives.

Hugging me one last time before walking out the door, Kelly whispered in my ear, "Remember! Talk to him, Hannah!"

Waving to the Lawsons as I slid into Seth's car, I knew I had to follow Kelly's advice. I needed some answers from Seth.

CHAPTER FIVE

A heart-to-heart talk was apparently not in Seth's plans. As we pulled back onto the road, he immediately started the conversation, keeping everything very superficial. I didn't even have the chance to discuss our visit with the Lawsons or thank him for going with me. It was almost as if he was afraid of a long, uncomfortable silence, but also afraid of what I might say if given the chance to choose a subject.

"I can't believe Christmas is only three days away! Are you planning to spend the holidays with your family?" he asked cheerfully.

"Yes. I need to head back up to Silver Springs. I called Abby earlier, but I know she'll be worried until she sees me in person. Our dad is coming Christmas Eve so we can all be together." Impulsively, I suddenly urged, "I wish you could come to the lodge with me. I mean, Abby will probably still think I'm crazy, but if you came, she'd have to believe me."

"I can't." Seth replied. "Remember, I have to work

tonight. Besides, you have the newspaper articles. That should be enough proof to convince her."

"Maybe you could come tomorrow? I know Abby and Tom would still like to meet you."

A look of pain shot across Seth's face. "I really can't, Hannah. I'm spending the holidays with Katherine's family. We're leaving after my shift tomorrow."

Katherine. And here we were at the subject I was most curious about. Taking a deep breath, I dove in before Seth could contribute another small-talk question.

"Seth, when exactly are you getting married?"

He cringed a little and mumbled, "Why do I get the feeling that you've been talking to Kelly?"

I waited. Seth ran a hand through his hair and sighed. "New Year's Eve. The wedding is New Year's Eve."

After the initial shock, I just felt numb. "Oh," was all I managed. I pretended sudden interest in the scenery flashing past us. Seeing that the scenery now consisted of mostly sound barrier walls on either side of the freeway, I knew I couldn't fake it forever. Still, I had a few blessed minutes while we drove in silence and my flittering thoughts focused.

"Congratulations, Seth." I finally responded, deciding to keep it simple. "I had no idea it was that soon." Closely inspecting my fingers in my lap, I debated with myself about whether I should just let the subject go or push my bad luck further.

Realizing this might be the last time I had a chance to get answers, I mustered courage and asked, "Can I ask you a personal question, Seth?"

Seth sighed, keeping his eyes on the road. "Honestly, I'd

probably rather you didn't, but go ahead and ask it anyway."

Ignoring his lackluster response, I rushed forward. "Are you in love with Katherine?"

Seth was silent for about a minute before he answered so quietly I had to strain to hear each word. "I do love Katherine. It may not be the fireworks kind of love in romance novels, but I care for her very much. We share a lot of history."

"That's what Kelly said."

Seth slowed the car down as we hit traffic. This trip was going to take longer than I thought. I tried to see around the traffic jam, hoping to be able to assess how much extra time it would cost us. I really wanted to be back at Silver Springs before nightfall.

Now slowing the car to almost a complete stop, Seth explained further, "Katherine and I dated off and on all through college and medical school. When I met you, we were off again and then for the next two years. Three years ago, we kind of got back together. We've been together ever since."

"I know it's none of my business, but what changed to get you back together." Not seeing an end of the traffic in sight, I figured I may as well hear the whole story.

"We were actually at Silver Springs for Christmas and…"

"Wait," I interrupted. "Do you go there a lot? The night we met, I'd wondered why you were even at the lodge."

"The previous owners of Silver Springs were old family friends of mine. When I came into the area for medical school, they invited me to spend some holidays with them since my family lived across the country at the time. Five years ago was the first Christmas I went. I spent Christmas there the next two years, but I also brought some other medical students who were displaced for the holidays."

"You haven't been back to the lodge recently?"

"No, we graduated and didn't go after George sold Silver Springs to your sister and her husband. Besides, that last Christmas kind of left a sour taste in everyone's mouth."

"Why? What happened?"

We had finally made it to where we could see the cause of the traffic. Two vehicles at the side of the road had obviously been in an accident. It didn't look serious, but the sleek silver sports car had definitely gotten the worst of it. The Ford truck looked unscathed, though it was a bit difficult to see through the layer of dirt encrusted around it. The vehicles weren't obstructing traffic, but the rubberneckers were. Irritated that we were delayed for such a foolish reason, I ignored my blatant hypocrisy, turning for my own accident inspection on the way past. Turning back to Seth, he answered my question.

"Everything actually happened before I got there. My best friend, Wayne Hawkins, was found with some drugs that had been stolen from the hospital. He was kicked out of medical school. He was gone before I even got to Silver Springs. Katherine and Wayne had been close, and she was really upset. That's kind of how we started talking and got back together. We both had to work through seeing someone we cared about, not to mention an incredibly talented physician, waste it all on drugs."

"That's so sad," I sympathized. "Were you able to stay in touch with Wayne. Is he doing okay now?"

"He only returned my call once after he left school. I

think he was embarrassed and didn't like to be reminded of what he'd lost. I probably could have tried harder to save the friendship, but I guess I felt betrayed. I was his best friend, yet I had no idea he had a drug problem. I certainly didn't know he'd been stealing drugs from the hospital. Last I heard, he was selling used cars. It was such a shame. Wayne was the top student in our class. He even had a dream research fellowship lined up at a premier hospital. He just had a few more months to go."

"What about Katherine?" I asked, thinking about Seth's story, "You said Katherine went to medical school with you, right? But she isn't a doctor. She's a nurse." In the city now, Seth expertly navigated the streets as we made our way back to my hotel.

"Katherine was a couple of years behind me in school. She is very intelligent, but she struggled in medical school. About two years ago, the stress and pressure got so bad that her parents insisted she quit. They paid for her to go to one of those exclusive spas that offer both physical and mental health amenities. It really worked for her. They taught her how to better cope with stress, and she was able to gain a healthier perspective. She decided not to return to medical school, and, her education considered, it was a relatively easy step for her to become a nurse."

"Does she enjoy being a nurse?" I asked, remembering the moody person I'd first met when looking for Seth.

"Yes, she does. Honestly, her not finishing medical school seems to bother me more than her. I was doing part of my residency out of state when she was having so much trouble. I've always wondered if she would have been able to finish if I'd been better able to support her."

"I'm sure Katherine doesn't feel that way."

"No, she's never said anything. She doesn't really like to talk about that time in her life. She's never really told me much about the spa and what they did to make such a difference for her. She's a private person in a lot of ways, but I know she is a stronger, better person for having worked through such difficulties."

"And now you're getting married," I stated, trying to inject only positive emotion into my words.

Pulling into the hotel parking lot, we were back to the same uncomfortable subject we started with. Seth turned the car off but made no move to get out. Instead, he sat with his hands on the steering wheel and his eyes focused ahead.

"Hannah, I don't want to give you the impression that you or that night didn't mean anything to me. I won't deny that we had an amazing connection." He grimaced. "Obviously, we still do. I spent two full years looking for you. It almost destroyed me. I had to give up and move on with my life. I had no idea I would ever see you again." Seth closed his eyes and whispered, "If I had only known…"

Tears burned behind my eyes and I struggled to swallow the painful knot in my throat.

Already knowing the answer, I asked the question anyway, "And now, it's too late?"

"Yes, it is. No matter what I feel; it doesn't change anything. It can't. I made a promise to Katherine when I asked her to marry me. I can't break that, especially after all she's been through. Everything's ready. The wedding is a little over a week away. You would not want the type of man who would break a commitment, Hannah. I committed to Katherine the day we got engaged, and I intend to stay committed to her for a lifetime."

As much as I hated the situation, I understood. Seth was a man of integrity, and I would never want him to do something that would violate a quality I so admired. I couldn't ask that of him.

"I understand," I whispered. "I should probably go now. Abby is expecting me tonight at the lodge."

I got out of the car, and Seth came around from the other side. We stood facing each other, but tried to avoid eye contact.

"I guess this is goodbye," I said. "Thank you for everything Seth. For five years ago. For listening and believing me yesterday. For taking me to the Lawsons. It's meant a lot to me. You've meant a lot to me."

Seth nodded. "Have a good Christmas. Good luck with school."

"Seth?" I asked. He finally raised his eyes and looked into mine. "I'm not going to see you again, am I?" It was a statement. I already knew.

"No, Hannah. I can't see you again. It wouldn't be fair to Katherine." He took a deep breath and shoved his hands in the pockets of his jeans. "You know how memories are often better than reality? Like if you run into someone you went to high school with, and you discover that he or she isn't nearly as nice, smart, or attractive as you remember. I always consoled myself with the thought that if I ever met the real Hannah, she wouldn't hold a candle to the Hannah I remembered, the one in my head."

Seth paused and looked in the direction of the bay before continuing in a soft, reflective voice. It was almost as if he were talking to himself. "I was wrong. The real Hannah is better than anything I remembered. You have blown away all my expectations. You are more beautiful, smarter, sweeter, and even funnier than I could have imagined. I can't look at you or even hear your voice and not feel."

By the time Seth finished speaking, his voice was cracking and his eyes begged me to understand. Wanting to comfort him, I reached my hand out to touch his cheek. He backed away, shying from my touch.

"Please, Hannah. Don't touch me." He closed his eyes, and I saw his throat working. "If you touch me, I'll forget everything. I'll take you in my arms and do what I've dreamt of doing for five years."

Feeling tears streaming down my face, I nodded and obediently put my hands in my coat pockets. "Goodbye, Seth."

"Goodbye, Hannah." And with that last strangled whisper, Seth turned, got in his car, and drove away. He didn't look back once.

CHAPTER SIX

I was disappointed to find that my recent bravery had not cured me of being a wimp. I couldn't handle the thought of driving by myself back up the mountain to Silver Springs, especially at night. I didn't want to face the memories, the terror of a repeat time travel mission, or the possibility of a serious panic attack that might get me hospitalized. So, since the doctor of my choice wouldn't be available should I need medical attention anyway, I curled up in the back seat of my car, cried my eyes out, then called my big sister.

Thankfully, Abby didn't ask a lot of questions. Not that she could have understood my answers anyway through the hiccuping shudders of my crying. Instead, she said if I could make it to Sonora, she and Tom would meet me there. Then she could ride with me to the lodge.

Before leaving San Francisco, I stopped at the nearest gas station. Slipping sunglasses over my bloodshot eyes, I braved the mini mart for supplies. There was only one thing that could calm me down enough to drive: chocolate. Thus armed with an embarrassing quantity — from M&M's to some fancy European chocolates — I made it to Sonora.

It was already pitch black outside by the time I reached Sonora and met Tom and Abby in the library parking lot. Abby hopped out of her own car and started toward my passenger side. I jumped out, wordlessly handed her the keys, and climbed in the passenger side myself. Abby's eyes widened with surprise. She was well aware of my phobia of other people's driving. I'd been a passenger in Abby's car before, but I don't think I'd ever been a passenger in my own.

As Abby started the SUV, she looked down at the empty candy wrappers.

"That bad, huh? Do you have any left?"

I dug around and found her a *Symphony* bar. She consented to munch in silence a few minutes, but I knew the candy bar wasn't *that* big. Soon she would start with the questioning. Leaning my head back and shutting my eyes for a few seconds before the interrogation, I actually fell asleep — another thing I never do when someone else is driving.

I woke up as Abby pulled up to the lodge and shut off the car. I was extremely grateful I had missed a second trip up the mountain in the dark.

After thanking Abby, I followed her into the kitchen where Tom stood in front of the refrigerator looking perplexed.

"Soup and cornbread, Sweetheart," Abby told Tom, answering his obvious question. "The lodgers have already eaten. I'll whip up the cornbread while Hannah fills us in."

Tom and Abby looked like a picture perfect couple

straight off the front cover of a magazine. Tom's tall, dark, ruggedly handsome type was the perfect compliment to Abby's cute, blond, girl-next-door type. I admit to an occasional bit of jealousy over my sister's good fortune in finding a husband who seemingly adored her. Not that I had ever been interested in Tom — he wasn't my type. But at least Abby had someone. Now, seeing them together felt a little like pouring lemon juice into the fresh wound of knowing Seth would never be mine.

"Abby told me what you said on the phone last night, Hannah." Tom said as he and I perched on bar stools watching Abby. "But I want to hear it again from you. Abby said you had a newspaper article that proves what happened?"

Retrieving the photocopied article from my purse, I showed Abby and Tom and then explained briefly what had happened since I last saw them. I didn't mention the conversation Seth and I had on the way back from the Lawson's house.

"This is incredible, Hannah!" Tom said when I had finished. "I see the evidence, but I'm still not sure I can believe it!"

That was not overly surprising to me. Tom was a great guy, but he was a pretty literal fellow who didn't really appreciate things that were outside his box of understanding.

"How long until supper is ready, Abby?" he asked suddenly.

Turning back from sliding the pan of cornbread into the oven, she answered, "About twenty minutes. Why?"

"I think I'll go hop on the Internet and see if I can find any more information about that accident or even other people who may have had time traveling experiences." Turning to me, he explained. "It's not that I don't believe you, Hannah. I just have a hard time wrapping my brain around it. Maybe if I get some more information, I can shift my paradigm back in place."

The second Tom's feet left the kitchen, Abby turned to me with flashing eyes. "OK, Hannah, spill it. Everything. I need details. Not the Reader's Digest version you gave Tom. What happened today that so upset you? Last night on the phone you were fine."

I told her about the conversation I'd had with Seth, how he was getting married in less than two weeks, even though he'd admitted having feelings for me. By the time I was finished, Abby was hugging me and handing me a Kleenex to wipe the tears that had apparently found a new water source.

"Now you probably really think I've lost it," I moaned, furiously wiping my eyes and blowing my nose. "I really only met the guy once, and suddenly I feel so strongly about him that I'm a blubbering mess at the thought of him being with someone else."

"I don't think you're crazy, Hannah. You and Seth shared something special."

"But?" I questioned. I knew there was a "but" coming. There usually was with Abby. Abby was always abundant in giving sympathy, but she was also always abundant in sharing her strong opinions as well. And in my opinion, especially where my life was concerned, Abby never seemed to lack an opinion.

"But..." Abby continued, "I do think some of your feelings may be magnified by a very traumatic and stressful few days. You've just been through an unbelievable and miraculous experience! It's completely normal for you to feel like you have developed strong feelings for a man who shared at least part of that experience with you."

Much to my annoyance, Abby had long ago developed a mothering attitude toward me. It really was unnecessary. Even though I'd never known our mother, our grandma had stepped in and, in many ways, filled the empty place in both of our lives. Besides, Abby was only two years older than me and had no memories of Mom either. I had tried, with limited success, to tolerate Abby's mothering, but at times it was hard to take.

Now, I took a deep breath and answered carefully, "I understand your point, Abby, but I really think it was more than just the after-effects of an adrenaline rush."

"But it doesn't really matter what it was, Hannah. You need to let go of both the time traveling experience and Seth. You won't be able to move on with your own life if you keep obsessing about what happened. Obviously, you and Seth weren't meant to be, or it would have worked out some way. He has Katherine, and there will be a different Prince Charming out there for you."

I knew Abby was just trying to help and encourage me, but sometimes having a smart, level-headed sister stunk! "I understand what you're saying, Abby, and I promise I'll work on it tomorrow, but today, I just want to wallow a bit more."

Abby smiled and gave me another hug. "That, I can understand. You have my permission to wallow as much as you want until midnight tonight. I'll even provide the hot fudge brownie sundaes for dessert."

Right then, the oven timer beeped. Tom, with impeccable timing, reentered the kitchen and found a place at the table.

Over steaming homemade chicken noodle soup and squares of moist cornbread, I asked Tom if he had found anything interesting on the Internet.

"No, not really. I didn't find out anything I didn't already know about the accident, and I found absolutely nothing on legitimate time traveling. I can look more later." Winking slyly at Abby, Tom added. "I just mainly wanted to give you ladies time to discuss some things I'm sure I didn't want to hear."

"Thanks, Tom," I said, smiling wryly. "Next time I need to have some girl talk with Abby, I'll remember to send you on some wild Internet search."

It was late after Abby and I finished wallowing in hot fudge brownie sundaes. Despite my nap on the ride to the lodge, I was still exhausted. I remembered no conscious thought after my head hit the pillow, and my sleep was blessedly dreamless. Waking to sunlight once again streaming through my window, I threw on my robe, and went down to find Abby once again in the kitchen.

"Happy Day Before Christmas Eve, Abby!" I announced cheerfully.

"Back at you, Sleepy Head." Abby retorted. "One of these days, I'm going to make you get up early and help me make breakfast for the lodgers."

"Get up early on my vacation? Abby, you're cruel. You'd better watch it, if you're too mean to me, I just might take back the very special Christmas present I got you."

"Very special, huh?" Abby asked, eyes sparkling. Abby loved a good surprise, especially when that surprise involved a present.

We continued bantering as I ate my breakfast of biscuits and gravy. Abby was an excellent cook, having had the patience to learn from our grandma. I, on the other hand, hadn't had the patience, and took more after our dad in cooking style. The microwave was my best friend. I was certainly not going to make any headway on losing that five pounds while indulging in Abby's cooking. I'd have gladly settled for the 130 on my driver's license, but I must have been feeling unusually optimistic the day I'd gotten it.

As I finished breakfast, we decided that baking dozens of cookies would be first on our list. Making desert was the closest thing to an exception in my bad cook persona. I was quite passable at making anything that involved a lot of butter and sugar.

After showering and dressing, Abby and I soon had the lodge smelling heavenly. It was nearing lunchtime, not that I was hungry. I had already liberally sampled fresh-from-the-oven cookies. The phone rang, and Abby answered it. It was a short call, and Abby was soon back to assembling sandwiches for the few guests still staying at the lodge.

"Who was on the phone," I asked conversationally as I smeared some white frosting over sugar cookies.

"Dad," she answered. "He called to say he thought he'd be here this afternoon around three."

"What?" I asked, confused. "I thought he had to work and wasn't going to be here until tomorrow."

A look of guilt crossed Abby's face before she quickly masked it, replying simply. "He was able to get off early."

"I suddenly had a sick feeling in the pit of my stomach, and I knew it wasn't the cookies. Pausing in the frosting of dozens of waiting sugar cookies, and turned to my sister. "What did you do, Abby?"

"Nothing. I mean when he called this morning, I might have mentioned what you had been going through the last few days."

"You did what? Abby, what exactly 'might you have mentioned?'"

I suddenly had the urge to start using my frosting-laden knife as a slingshot. Seeing Abby with white and green frosting dotting her hair and smearing her face would do my heart good. Overcoming temptation, I set the knife down carefully, pointedly awaiting an explanation.

"OK, so I told him about your whole time traveling rescue and your visit with Seth and the Lawsons, but it was very brief. I didn't fill in the details." At my shocked, accusing stare, she continued. "Don't look at me like I just committed the unpardonable sin, Hannah. He's our father. He had the right to know."

"But you had no right to tell him," I seethed. "It's my life. It was my business to tell. I didn't want to tell him over the phone, and I certainly didn't want him rushing up here to help his insane daughter."

"He doesn't think you're insane."

"How do you know? What did he say?"

"He was actually kind of quiet. You know Dad gets that way when he's stressed or upset. I'm not saying he was upset, he just asked if I had seen the newspaper article about the accident. He started to ask some more questions, but then stopped and said he'd ask you himself. I didn't know at the time that he was going to get here early to ask them."

Seeing my expression hadn't relented, Abby defended. "Oh, come on, Hannah. There was no harm done."

"No harm done? Dad took off work and is, right now, probably breaking every speed limit trying to get here and make sure I'm okay. You know he's worried."

"It'll be fine, Hannah."

"That isn't good enough, Abby. Even if things are 'fine,' that doesn't change the fact that you told something that wasn't your business to tell. What are you? Five years old that you have to go tattle on me to Dad the first chance you got?"

Abby turned on me, her own eyes now flashing angrily. "Knock it off, Hannah! I'm done with your self-absorption and your rude conversation. I'm not the one who needs to *grow up*!"

Grabbing the tray of sandwiches, Abby pointedly marched out of the room to deliver them to the dining room table. Over her shoulder, she flung one final accusation, "Next time God sends you on a time traveling mission, maybe you should pay attention to more than just the unavailable eye candy. If you learned some manners, maybe you could actually find a guy who cared!"

As she left the room, I untied my apron and furiously threw it on the counter. "I'm not done talking to you!" I yelled back at her.

It had been a long time since Abby had made me this furious. My hands were shaking with anger. How dare she tell Dad! Why couldn't she just butt out and let me make my own decisions?

Moving to follow her into the dining room, I continued yelling. "You owe me an apology, Abigail Stevens!

Walking through the kitchen doorway, I stopped in my tracks like I'd been turned to stone.

Abby wasn't in the dining room. In fact, the table wasn't even set for lunch.

"Abby?" I called loudly, confused. "Abby, where are you?"

"Who are you looking for?" A voice asked from the doorway that exited into the front hall. Looking up, I saw a tall man with wavy brown hair and a friendly smile. I thought I had already met all of the current lodgers, but apparently I hadn't. I didn't remember having seen him before.

"My sister Abby," I replied. When he still looked confused, I rephrased, "Abigail Stevens?"

"Is she a guest here? Maybe she hasn't arrived yet. I know the rest of the people from my party are arriving later today."

I started to inform him that Abigail Stevens was the owner of Silver Springs, and she hadn't mentioned any other guests arriving for the holidays. Instead, I paused, and looked again at the dining room. It was different than I remembered and not just because the table wasn't set. That picture on the wall was one Abby would never have on her property, and the carpet under the table was threadbare and atrocious. The bad feeling I had was starting to turn to nausea.

"And you are?" I asked, changing my tactic.

"Wayne Hawkins," the man replied, flashing a smile of even white teeth a dentist would envy.

Wayne Hawkins? Wasn't that the name of Seth's best friend? Where was I? Or, maybe more importantly, *when* was I?

I felt the blood drain from my face.

This couldn't be happening! Not again!

I started to sway.

Wayne grabbed me. "Maybe you should sit down," he said, gently guiding me to a chair.

"I'm sure your sister will show up," he encouraged. "Is she a medical student?"

"No," I answered.

What was I going to do? I couldn't even ask Wayne questions without making him suspicious. He'd surely think I was insane! I really didn't need to be locked up here, wherever here was.

I needed to pretend like I belonged. Nobody could suspect anything. It was too dangerous. I had to figure out when I was and how to get back home.

"I'm just feeling a little faint," I said simply. "Some water or juice might bring me out of it."

"Oh, certainly," Wayne replied, "I was just heading to the kitchen to scrounge up something to eat for lunch. I could bring you something," he offered.

No!" I said, panic slicing through me. "I'll just come

with you. I'm feeling better now." There was no way I was going to let Wayne out of my sight. I didn't know who or what I'd run into next.

In the kitchen, Wayne rummaged through the refrigerator, stacking juice and sandwich ingredients on the counter.

"George said we were welcome to raid the refrigerator as long as we made our own meals." Wayne explained. "He really doesn't do much as far as meals for guests since Elsie died. But, it was awfully nice of him to let us come up for the holidays anyway."

I remembered George from the night of the accident. He was the one who'd opened the front door. He was also the one Seth had said was the previous owner of the lodge and his family friend. My brain was frantically scrounging up memories. I also remembered an older woman helping the night of the accident. She must have been George's wife, Elsie. So, if she was dead, then I figured I must be in some time frame between the accident and my current time when Abby and Tom owned Silver Springs. I know Seth mentioned that he and his friends went to Silver Springs for two Christmases after we met, I just didn't know which one this was.

"Do you want a sandwich?" Wayne asked.

"No, I'm not really feeling hungry. I'll probably just have some apple juice." After pouring myself a glass, I perched on a bar stool and watched Wayne assemble a sandwich a chef would be proud of.

Watching the culinary masterpiece take shape, I calculated this was probably the first year after Seth and I met. I knew that the second year was when Wayne got kicked out of school for drugs. In my opinion, there was no way this friendly, good-natured, down-to-earth guy could be into drugs. The only thing that made sense was if something major happened in his life between now and then.

"So you're meeting your sister here for the holidays?" Wayne questioned as he mixed together his own special mustard that included at least two spices I didn't even recognize.

'Yes, I kind of already expected her to be here." I admitted truthfully.

"I'm sure she'll…" Wayne never finished his thought. The second *she* walked in, Wayne's eyes and attention were entirely focused on Katherine Colson, Seth's future fiancé.

Katherine's glance slid over me and rested on Wayne, not bothering to even acknowledge my presence.

"Hi, Katherine," Wayne said, his cheerful voice contrasting the intense look in his eyes. "Do you want some lunch?"

Katherine made a face. "I'm not hungry. Where is everyone else? I didn't go home for Christmas because you told me that everyone was going to be here and we'd have a great time."

"Some are down in the den area. Everyone else should be arriving this afternoon. I, for one, am glad you decided to join us."

I wanted to roll my eyes like a teenager. Wayne was practically drooling over Katherine. The soft tone of voice, the puppy dog look that begged for attention, the intense focus of his eyes as they studied her face — everything screamed "Love me back!" But Katherine was cool, indifferent.

She looked pretty much the same as when I met her in the future: a trim, statuesque figured topped with beautiful wavy blond locks with every last hair in place. I supposed her face would also be considered classically beautiful with high cheekbones and full lips, but I found the planes of her face to be rather harsh and her expression cold and superior. Today there seemed to be a tiredness around her eyes that even her expensive eye makeup couldn't hide. Remembering what Seth had said about her difficulty with medical school, I figured the fatigue and maybe at least some of her bad attitude was from this stress.

Wayne suddenly appeared to remember my presence and turned. "Katherine, I'd like you to meet…" Here he paused, confused as he probably realized he'd never actually asked me my name.

"Hannah," I supplied.

"She and her sister are here for the holidays," he finished.

Katherine glanced at me, but still didn't acknowledge my presence. Turning back to Wayne and folding her arms in front of her, she returned to her previous complaining. "So what's the plan, Wayne? Are we just going to wait around all day?"

"No. I think a bunch of us are planning to decorate George's Christmas tree and watch some movies this afternoon in the den. You're welcome to join us."

"I don't know if I can handle the excitement," Katherine

replied sarcastically.

"Come on, Katherine, you knew before you came that this wasn't going to be a wild party trip. We all just want to relax, de-stress, and have a nice, traditional Christmas, even if we aren't able to be with our families." When Katherine didn't respond, Wayne added hopefully, "We're going skiing tomorrow, and we have snowmobiling planned for this weekend. Those should be exciting."

Katherine sighed and acquiesced. "The den, right? I guess I'll come and join you guys. It's not like I have anything better to do."

Wayne's grin rivaled that of an eight year old who had just won free tickets to Disneyland.

I was tired of listening to their exclusive and rather ridiculous conversation. But I had nowhere else to go.

Chocolate. I needed chocolate. In a house this size, there had to be some chocolate somewhere. As Wayne and Katherine continued talking, I began a methodical search of the cupboards.

Wayne lowered his voice and was now speaking about something that was obviously more personal in nature. I would say that I didn't intentionally eavesdrop, but that might be considered a lie. I could grudgingly admit that enjoying other people's business must have been a family trait that Abby and I were genetically predisposed for. However, my nosiness was usually for informational purposes only; I didn't get involved. Abby, on the other hand, didn't care as much about information as she did about getting involved. And, unfortunately, it usually seemed my business was her favorite to be involved in.

It wasn't difficult to follow the conversation as I searched the cupboards. While Wayne's voice remained too soft for me to hear, Katherine's did not. She hadn't bothered to acknowledge my presence earlier, why should she start worrying about it now?

Wayne said something to which Katherine responded, eyes flashing angrily, "Back off, Wayne! I already told you no. It's nice to see that you trust me so little!"

I heard the soothing tone of Wayne's voice, but couldn't make out the words.

"Just let it go, okay?" Katherine responded, slightly mollified. "Don't ask me again."

After Wayne spoke again, Katherine nodded stiffly, "I'll let you know." Taking a deep breath, she nodded toward his sandwich. "I'll let you get back to your lunch. I'm going to run upstairs to my room a few minutes. I'll meet you back down in the den?"

"Sure," Wayne responded, his voice now normal and his friendly grin back in place. "See you in a few!"

Finally! Standing on tiptoes, my hand connected with a bag of chocolate chips in the back of a cupboard.

Wayne finished his sandwich as I perched back on the bar stool and tried to munch away my stress. Finally completing his creation, Wayne sat across from me and dug in.

I idly wondered what he and Katherine had been discussing, but I didn't ask. Instead, we made small talk, mostly covering Wayne's unusual talent and interest in gourmet cuisine.

"You're welcome to come join us in the den," Wayne invited after finishing his sandwich.

Not having anything else to do with myself, I gratefully accepted. There were four others in the den when we arrived. Two guys were carting boxes of Christmas decorations over to a large tree in the corner where two girls giggled as they discovered ornaments and a hodgepodge of other decorations inside.

I introduced myself and joined the girls. Natalie, Sicily, and I soon had the tree shimmering with a myriad of lights and ornaments from decades past.

"Wow," said the dark-haired girl named Natalie. "George has quite an assortment of ornaments here. Some of these might even be antiques." She held up a small glass bell etched with the date 1939.

"Yeah," I replied, "those ornaments that don't belong in the trash might definitely be antiques." Holding up a torn one that was obviously made from an egg carton, I continued, "You can have this lovely one right here, Natalie, for a mere two hundred bocks."

Suppressed mirth in her eyes, Sicily gasped, "Did you say 'bocks?'"

"Yes," I replied in all seriousness. "The currency of poultry. Considering the egg carton and all. You know — bock, bock, bock!"

Everyone burst into fits of giggles. After that, we had a difficult time finishing the tree between gales of laughter, as we kept coming up with sales pitches and prices for the misfit ornaments.

Under stress, I usually had two defaults — fall to pieces and cry or perch on the edge of hysteria and laugh. When was I? What was I supposed to do? What would I tell these people when they started asking questions? How could I get back to my own time? I didn't have the answers and I couldn't fall to pieces — so I laughed.

About midway through decorating, Katherine glided into the room. With a smile on her face and a friendly greeting, she immediately joined us and began energetically joining in the silliness. At Katherine's bright-eyed smile and wave at Wayne, I watched him literally do a double take. Apparently, I wasn't the only one who was floored by Katherine's dramatic attitude adjustment.

The rest of the medical students, about eight more, arrived just in time to ooh and aah over our finished project. After settling in, everyone started watching a movie. Now that the laughter was over and everyone else was occupied, I was at loose ends and given way too much time to think.

Even though the movie was considered a 'new release' in this time, I had already seen it and the new release sequel in my own time. The sequel was a mistake, as most sequels are. It had been so bad that it kind of ruined the first one for me, and I had no desire to watch it.

Besides that, I couldn't relax enough to sit down and watch a movie even if I'd wanted to. I was wound up so tight I was fast approaching nervous wreck status. When I'd previously gone back in time, I hadn't been aware of it until after it had happened. Also in my previous experience, urgent and traumatic events had happened that needed my attention and kept my mind occupied. Now, there was nothing to do. I saw no one who needed my help — no need to put on the Super Hannah suit.

Instead, left to my own thoughts, I was now fully aware that I was stuck. If this was a mission from God, what exactly was I supposed to do? And, I had no idea how to get back to my own time.

I couldn't confide in anyone. I had no proof. I didn't think that the line, "I've come from the future," would be well received in a room full of medical students. The only person who might believe and help me was Seth, but I had no idea when he would arrive.

To mask my restless pacing, I pretended to browse the books on the shelves lining the walls. No one seemed to notice. Katherine, appearing to have found her appetite as well as a dose of hospitality, returned from the kitchen with a variety of snacks to share.

Loud voices echoed from the hallway. I looked up. Everyone else was engrossed in the movie and didn't seem to have heard. The door to the den opened. Two fierce-looking older men walked in, letting the door bang shut behind them. The movie viewers jumped and turned so suddenly it was comical.

The scowls on their faces of the men at the door made me want to duck and cover, and I didn't even know them.

"Mr. Hawkins, turn that blasted thing off," the tall one ordered curtly. He was slender with an erect posture and silver hair. He would normally look very gentlemanly and scholarly, but the intense displeasure in his eyes and expression on his face masked that.

"Why, Dr. James and Dr. Stockburg, what a surprise!" Wayne managed while hurrying to comply. "We didn't expect to see you here!"

"It isn't a trip for pleasure, I assure you," the doctor replied stiffly.

When the movie was off, the one I assumed was Dr. James scanned the room, making sure he had everyone's attention. "I take it everyone is here?" he questioned.

At Wayne's confirmation, Dr. James continued, "Good, then I'll get right to the point. Dr. Stockburg and I came all the way up here on a matter of urgent business. Someone in this room stole drugs from the hospital last night, and we intend to find out who that person is."

In that instant, I knew exactly *when* I was.

CHAPTER SEVEN

A shocked silence followed the doctor's announcement. My eyes swung to Wayne, trying to detect any guilt in his expression. His eyes were on Katherine's, but I couldn't read the look. Maybe he was wordlessly pleading for her understanding.

A student named Richard was the first to speak. "Dr. James, how do you know it was one of us? There are a lot of other medical students who work at the hospital, not to mention all the other nurses and staff who would have access to medications."

"You are correct," the doctor replied. "However, this wasn't just a one-time occurrence. The theft has been going on for several months. We have been monitoring it, and finally, last night, we felt we had enough evidence to narrow down the list of suspects. All of the thefts have occurred when most of the people in this room have been on duty. It's natural you would create friendships with the people you go to school and share a shift with. When we asked around and discovered that all of you were spending Christmas here, we decided this couldn't wait. We want to have this issue settled before the holidays. Besides, time is a factor in the investigation."

"What do you mean, 'time is a factor,'" asked Sicily.

Dr. James nodded to Dr. Stockburg, and, for the first time, the shorter man spoke up. His appearance looked almost ridiculous standing next to the stately Dr. James. Dr. Stockburg was considerably shorter and rounder than his colleague. As he cleared his throat, Dr. Stockburg self-consciously pushed his thick, dark glasses up on his nose and adjusted his black, furry toupee.

"All of you signed paperwork, both when you entered medical school and when you began your internships with the hospital." Here he stopped and removed a thick sheaf of papers from his briefcase. "Among other things, these documents give us the authority to perform both random and targeted drug testing. In short, we can order drug testing of anyone, for any reason, at any time. We are now going to exercise this authority."

Dr. James broke in and explained, "Due to the kind and quantity of drugs that have been stolen over the last few months, we believe the individual responsible intended them for personal use and not for distribution. Of course, we could be wrong. But we still believe that the wisest and fairest course of action would be to have all of the possible suspects, all of you, drug tested. We brought the testing kits and, since we know what to look for, Dr. Stockburg and I can analyze the results within an hour. We'll have our answers today. Since we already have everyone's written consent, we just need you each to take a kit so we can get started."

"Not all of the potential suspects are here, though, Dr. James," Richard interrupted. "Seth McAllister is coming to spend the holidays here as well. Isn't he supposed to arrive tonight?"

"Seth McAllister isn't on our list of suspects. He sometimes works a different schedule than the rest of you. For instance, he was working today while the rest of you had it off. He was not working last night or at the time of some of the other thefts."

"Any other questions?" Dr. James continued, "So, without further ado, we'll get started. That is, unless the person responsible wants to just save us all the trouble and confess."

I scanned the tense faces of the silent medical students. Most of them were standing, shifting their feet nervously and making eye contact with no one. Natalie and Sicily sat on the couch, staring blankly at the Christmas tree everyone had so joyfully decorated. Katherine was sitting in a chair, studying the floor and rubbing her arms like she was cold. She looked up and saw Wayne watching her intently.

Wayne's expression looked tortured, undecided for a moment. He must have found the strength he was looking for in Katherine's face because, a moment later, he softly cleared his throat.

"It was me." He said quietly. "I took the drugs."

To say that the two doctors were shocked would have been an understatement. Dr. James' mouth literally fell open for at least five seconds before he shut it with a click.

Dr. Stockburg sputtered, "Mr. Hawkins, I've supervised you myself! You must forgive me for saying that I don't believe you."

Wayne shrugged, then said, "You never said the name of the drug that was taken." He then gave the name of a drug I didn't recognize and could never hope to pronounce.

"Follow me, Wayne." Dr. James sighed. "I have permission to use the owner's office."

The three men were gone less than five minutes, during which the lounge resembled a wax museum. Not one person spoke or even seemed to move.

Returning from the office, Wayne stopped in his tracks. He could not help but read the expressions of shock and hurt plainly written on his friends' faces.

He rubbed a hand across his haggard face, then spoke brokenly. "The doctors were kind enough to agree to not press charges if I left school quietly. Obviously, I won't be staying with you guys for the holidays. I've got to go up and pack." Before exiting the room, Wayne scanned the sorrowful faces once again and said in a hoarse whisper, "I'm so sorry!"

As soon as he left, confused voices and tears were released as everyone tried to make sense of what had just happened. In the mayhem, I watched as Katherine, with an anguished expression, slipped away and followed Wayne upstairs. Curious, and seeing no reason to reign in my nosiness now, I followed too.

Rounding the corner into the upstairs hallway, I stopped when I heard hushed voices. I could clearly hear Wayne and Katherine at the entrance to what I assumed was his room.

"I can't let you do this, Wayne!" I heard Katherine say through her tears.

"It's already done," Wayne replied stiffly. "I wish you

would have been honest with me and listened the first time."

Katherine's sobbing hiccups filled the silence.

Wayne sighed. "Just give it to me, Katherine. All of it. I have to return it."

I heard a shaking sound as Katherine passed him something.

"I don't understand why you're doing this," Katherine said brokenly.

"You know why, Katherine. Or you should know why by now. I'm doing it for you."

Katherine's sobs became muffled, and I imagined Wayne was holding her.

Inching closer, I heard Wayne whisper, "I'll be alright. Don't worry about me. Just don't waste your chance. Not many people get a third."

"I won't," Katherine promised quietly.

"Now, I need to finish packing and you need to get back down with the others before someone gets suspicious." Wayne said, obviously trying to sound cheerful. "I'll call you in a few days. I hope you don't mind waiting to get your Christmas present from me."

I ducked into an open bathroom as a visibly upset Katherine came out of Wayne's room. Watching as she bypassed the stairs, I saw her enter what I assumed was her own room instead of following Wayne's instructions and joining the others downstairs.

Putting together everything Seth had told me about Katherine's history along with what I had witnessed and heard today, it didn't tax my brain too much to figure out what was really going on.

Slipping out of the bathroom and through the doorway into Wayne's room, I shut the door softly. Being a rather accomplished eavesdropper myself, I knew better than to leave a door even slightly ajar on a private conversation. Turning, I met Wayne's surprised gaze as he looked up from his open suitcase.

"I know the drugs are Katherine's." I announced without preamble.

Seeing the angry, rebellious light in his eyes, I held up my hand to stop his denial and hurried to explain. "I'd have to be pretty dense not to figure it out, Wayne. You're obviously in love with her. You and I both saw the night and day difference in her behavior from the kitchen to the lounge. She probably downed some pills in between. My guess is that you somehow knew about her problem beforehand and then, when it was discovered, you decided to take the bullet for her in order to protect the woman you love."

I watched the fight drain out of Wayne's eyes. He slumped down on the bed and put his hands over his eyes.

"It wasn't obvious. You just apparently have some super-human perceptive skills or something."

I didn't bother to admit that those super-human skills involved future knowledge and a keen talent for eavesdropping.

"But, you're right," he continued. "About everything." He sighed and lifted his eyes to look at me. "At the hospital a couple weeks ago, I caught Katherine stealing some prescription pills when we were on duty. That's how I made an educated guess about what specifically was stolen. I confronted her about it. She told me that she had never done it before, this was the first time. She was really upset, saying she had been under a lot of stress and was just trying to find something to take the edge off. I told her I wouldn't turn her in as long as she never did it again and she got some help. She promised. Obviously, she didn't tell the truth about that being the first time or about keeping her promises and getting help."

"And you think that will be different now?" I questioned. "Now that you've sacrificed yourself and given her another chance to keep the promises she couldn't keep before?"

Wayne's look was anguished. "I don't know," he admitted honestly. "But I couldn't sit there and watch her humiliated and have everything taken from her."

"You'd rather it be done to you."

"Yes," he replied with conviction. "I can recover. I don't know that Katherine could."

After thinking for a moment, I spoke. "I think you're underestimating Katherine. Some people never show or develop strength because they never need to. You're protecting her is really not doing her any favors. She'll be more likely to get help if you let her face the consequences for her actions. She has a drug problem that no one but you and I know about. You're the one who needs to have the strength to *let* Katherine fall and prove she can get back up."

"But she'll lose everything. She'll be kicked out of school and lose everyone's respect. Her family is very well known. There might even be a public scandal."

"All those problems are insignificant compared to the problems she might have if she doesn't get help. Again, I think you're underestimating her. I get the impression that Katherine's family is quite wealthy." At Wayne's nod, I continued. "Think about it, Wayne. If they have any influence, they will have the whole dismissal from medical school swept under the carpet. No one but the people here, her closest friends, will even know. Then, they'll send her to one of those exclusive 'spas' that is actually a drug rehab center for the wealthy."

"You really think so?" Wayne asked, a glimmer of hope in his voice.

"Absolutely. You know her family; what do you think they'll do?" Remembering Seth's words and obvious naiveté about Katherine's life-changing spa visit, I smiled and continued. "I think they'll circulate the story that Katherine was under a lot of stress and has taken a vacation at a wonderful spa where they offer both physical and mental health rejuvenating amenities. She'll relax and learn ways to manage her stress. She'll come back home to more respect for her Zen-likeness."

Wayne didn't say anything at all. He continued staring at the carpet like he hadn't heard a word I said. I blew out a frustrated breath and tried a different tactic. "Obviously, Wayne, I can't make you do anything. If you want to protect Katherine and throw away your career as a doctor, that's your choice. I just ask that you think about it a little. From what I hear, you are very gifted and will probably be an exceptional doctor. You're well-liked and at the top of your class, right?

Ignoring his shrug, I continued. "I also hear that Katherine has struggled through medical school, and now she's floundering under the stress. Even if she somehow manages to make it to graduation with a drug problem, she won't ever be the doctor you will. Think about the lives you could affect as a doctor versus those that Katherine could."

Wayne looked up at me with a sardonic smile. "Stop while you're ahead, Hannah. You're losing steam. Do you think I'd really go for the 'think of the greatest good' argument?"

"You're right. I usually hate the 'greatest good' line of thinking too, but, in this case, the greatest good also includes Katherine's greatest good."

"And that's what you have me considering," Wayne admitted, but then I watched the light of hope fade from his eyes. "It's too late. I've already admitted the drugs were mine. I now have them in my possession. They'll never even believe me if I say I didn't take them."

"That shouldn't be too hard to prove," I said confidently. "Just offer to take the drug test. They can test everyone if they want, but you and I both know Katherine's will come back positive." Seeing his reluctance, I added, "But, I don't think that will be necessary. The minute the doctors start talking to her, she'll probably break down and admit everything."

"I don't know. Katherine can be a pretty good actress sometimes."

Knowing all I'd seen and heard of Katherine, I would have termed her fake and deceptive, but I wasn't going to argue the point. "I still doubt she'll let it go as far as the drug test. She knows what it'll show."

Looking very stressed and uncertain, Wayne asked. "Can you give me a few minutes to think about this, Hannah? Everyone is waiting downstairs, and I need to process things alone."

"Sure, Wayne. Just let me know if I can help."

As I walked out the door, I cringed a little as I heard

Wayne say with a tinge of sarcasm, "No, I think you've helped enough."

CHAPTER EIGHT

BACK downstairs, everyone was waiting for the next installment of today's drama. One group was involved in a discussion around the Christmas tree, while another group, led by Natalie, was having a discussion with the two doctors. Katherine was curled on a couch looking miserable.

After listening in for a few minutes, I sincerely wished for earplugs. Natalie, who was interested in obstetrics, was held in rapt attention as the two doctors described and debated the latest techniques in performing an emergency c-section. I had never been interested in becoming a physician of any sort. I just didn't have the stomach for it. I'd take a test tube over an actual person any day.

Wayne was surprisingly quick in coming downstairs. Every eye in the room riveted on him as he approached the two doctors. With relief, I noted that he was not carrying his suitcase.

"Dr. James, Dr. Stockburg, may I have a word with you?" Wayne asked. As they nodded and moved to George's office, Wayne stopped at Katherine's chair. He spoke softly, but every syllable was heard in the silent room. "Katherine, you probably better come too."

Katherine responded with a shocked look, but immediately followed the others.

There wasn't much talk as everyone waited on pins and needles. Fortunately, the wait was a lot shorter than I expected. Before a full ten minutes had passed, the office door opened.

Dr. James walked to the center of the room and paused for a solid thirty seconds. "I'm not sure what to tell all of you," he said finally, speaking with uncharacteristic hesitation. "You have a right to know because you've already been privy to some misinformation, but there are other individual privacy issues as well. As such, I'm not going to answer any questions, and I ask that hereafter you let the subject drop for all the concerned parties."

Again, he paused before continuing, "Despite being guilty of a temporary lapse in judgment, Mr. Wayne Hawkins has been cleared of any wrong doing. He was not involved in any drugs or theft from the hospital. He will continue as a medical student with the rest of you. Miss Katherine Colson, on the other hand, has decided to join her family for the holidays. She is making arrangements to that end right now and will be leaving shortly. That will be all."

After his speech, a red-eyed Katherine emerged from the office and wordlessly headed upstairs to her room. In world record breaking time, she was back down with two suitcases and a garment bag. Saying a quick goodbye to everyone while avoiding any eye contact with a visibly despondent Wayne, Katherine moved to leave with the two doctors.

Before walking through the front door, her eyes seemed to search for and collide with mine from across the room. I don't know how, but she must have figured out my involvement in Wayne's reversal. I had never felt or seen such smoldering hatred in one look. Though I stood right in front of the fireplace, goose bumps spotted my arms. I knew I had made an enemy.

I tried to shrug it off. The Katherine of the future hated me. Why shouldn't the Katherine of the past hate me too?

As soon as the door shut, Sicily announced with false gaiety that it was dinner time. Everyone pitched in with unusual gusto to get dinner on the table. I think everyone was relieved to forgo the silence of not knowing what to say or the equally uncomfortable possibility of rehashing the drama. Instead, chicken was grilled, courtesy of George Foreman, salad was tossed, and fruit was chopped.

Wayne even pulled it together and contributed fabulous homemade cheddar cheese biscuits. He had obviously never made them for Katherine. If he had, she surely would have fallen into his arms and not let go. What woman wouldn't want a handsome doctor who could also cook like a five star chef? As it was, several of the ladies present seemed to be vying to put their name on Wayne's waiting list.

No one mentioned Katherine or said anything to Wayne about his bizarre behavior at any point in the evening. Would this group of friends never talk about what had just happened? I really had to admire the honor and respect they showed if they were really planning on adhering to Dr.

James's instructions about letting the subject drop.

After supper, someone suggested we play some board games. I was normally very competitive and loved board games, but not today. The drama of Wayne's situation had been distracting, but now the panic was rising once again. Hours had passed and I still had no clue what to do or how to get back where I was supposed to be.

I knew there was no way I'd be able to focus on a group game while pretending that I belonged and was having fun. As Wayne turned from where he stood by the fireplace, I saw in his face the same aversion about joining the gathering around the Yahtzee board.

"Do you play chess?" Wayne asked me.

"A little," I admitted. Wayne was right. Playing a quiet game of chess would be far better than a rousing game of Yahtzee or whatever else they came up with next. And it would give us a good excuse to stay away from the others while not appearing upset and antisocial.

Wayne found a chess board and placed it on the coffee table in front of the fire. As he arranged the white pieces on his side of the board, he spoke quietly

"Hannah, I'm not ready to say thank you."

"I wouldn't expect you to," I replied.

I knew Wayne was probably waging a fierce battle with his guilt and thoughts. I had the advantage of knowing a little of how things would have turned out if he had sacrificed himself for Katherine. I knew Katherine would have never graduated medical school anyway and that he would have lost his friends and career. I couldn't picture

Wayne as a satisfied or even successful car salesman. I had complete confidence that Wayne did the right thing; Wayne didn't have that confidence.

After that one exchange, neither of us said anything else. I had probably said too much about his personal business today anyway. Any reassurances from me probably wouldn't have been received well. We focused on the game instead. I could tell that Wayne was a decent chess player, and I was thankful that my dad had taught me when I was little.

After at least twenty minutes of back-and-forth exchanges, Wayne stood and stretched.

"I think I may need a break," he said. "My mind is feeling a little fuzzy."

"Sure," I said, standing and stretching as well. "I have you checkmated in three moves anyway."

Wayne stared at me. "I get the feeling you're a lot better at chess than you let on."

I shrugged. "My dad always said I was good, but, he's my dad; he doesn't count." Then smiling a little, I continued, "I guess I'll always be a nerd at heart."

"Well, then, you're in good company," Wayne responded as he lounged back on the couch, hands behind his head and eyes closed. "I'll demand a rematch at a later date."

Knowing that I had been dismissed, I left Wayne to his rest and went back to the table. One end was still occupied by an extremely fierce game of *Pit*. Grabbing a pen that had been left over from a previous game, I confiscated the small pile of unused paper napkins from dinner and found a seat at the opposite end.

I tried to calm my tumbling thoughts as I drew. But it wasn't working. It was getting late, and I didn't even have a room in this time frame to go to. Things were going to become even more complicated when others began noticing that I had no bed, no luggage, no transportation, no money, and no clue how to get any.

My heart accelerated. The pen in my hand was slippery from my suddenly sweaty palm. What was I going to do?

God, you helped me rescue that family last time, I prayed, could you give me a little help with this one too?

"When is Seth supposed to get here?" Richard asked across the table.

My head snapped up from my doodles.

"Sometime tonight," another guy named John answered. "He was going to drive up after his shift today, but I noticed it was snowing outside. That might delay him some."

"Poor, Seth," said Natalie. "He's probably going to be really upset about Katherine."

"You know, Seth," Sicily replied. "It might be just what's needed to get him and Katherine back together again."

"So, has he given up looking for his mystery woman?" Richard sneered. Judging from his current comments and his mention of Seth being a possible suspect to the doctors earlier, I got the distinct impression that there was no love lost between Richard Borley and Seth McAllister.

"I'm sure he's given up by now," said Natalie confidently. "It's been like two years, right?"

"I swear I've been watching the man slowly go insane looking for a figment of his imagination. If he hasn't snapped out of it by New Year's, I think I might try to find a way to give an anonymous tip that the guy needs a psych evaluation before he should be allowed to graduate," Richard said.

"Richard, that's awful!" Sicily accused indignantly.

"I'd be careful if I were you, Richard. You're on dangerous ground," a smiling John said. "I've found that, mystery woman or not, all of the ladies around here think that Seth McAllister is the best thing since sliced bread. If you start messing with him, you'd better be prepared to have some of the best female minds in the country combing through your past with a fine toothed comb. I'm sure they won't find any reason you shouldn't be a well-respected physician, right?"

Natalie, Sicily, and the others were all smiling gleefully. Richard looked uncomfortable, his face turning red even though he tried to shrug nonchalantly.

"I'm not worried," Richard said unconvincingly. "What was that girl's name he's looking for anyway? Wasn't it something common like Sarah?

"Hannah," Natalie replied. "I think it was Hannah."

"I told you it was common. Hasn't that been like the number one name for the last ten years?" Richard said. "There are millions of Hannahs. Speaking of which," pointing to me across the table, he called, "what did you say your name was?"

"Hannah," I answered honestly. "My name is Hannah."

Wayne's head popped off the couch like a fishing bobber, but nobody else seemed to have heard me for, at that exact moment, two guys excitedly rushed into the room.

"George found the cues for the pool table!" one of them announced. "Are you up for the challenge, Richard?"

Grinning recklessly, Richard stood, "I think the question is, Todd, are *you* up for the challenge?"

With whistles and hoots, the room emptied as the men left to commence their epic battle, and everyone else went to witness it. Wayne was the only other occupant left in the room. He was staring at me.

He stood from the couch and walked toward me, studying my features with a shocked and unbelieving look on his face.

"There's no way… You can't be…" Wayne struggled to phrase a complete thought. Finally, he swallowed and asked, "Are you Seth's Hannah?"

Feeling shaky and nervous, but not knowing what else to do, I simply nodded.

Wayne looked dazed. Running a hand through his hair, he started rambling, "I don't know why I didn't see it before. You look exactly like he described. Of course, I don't know that I fully believed his story about your disappearance. But after everything that's happened today…" He paused in his monologue as his face took on a glow like the sun coming from behind the clouds. "I've got to tell Seth!"

"I thought he was coming here tonight anyway," I said, confused about Wayne's sudden urgency and excitement.

"He is, but he won't believe who's waiting here. Maybe he's not even started up the mountain yet and I can catch him on his cell. I've got to try. He'd never forgive me if I didn't tell him the minute I found out it was you. The guy has practically gone insane looking for you."

Wayne's transformation was incredible. He'd gone from the sullen brooding of a guilt-ridden man to the giddy excitement of a child anticipating Christmas morning. His grin stretched from ear to ear, and his movements were frantic and jerky. Pulling out his own cell phone, he found he didn't have reception.

"I'll have to use George's land line," he said, moving to make a dash for the door. Skidding to a stop like a cartoon character, Wayne suddenly whirled back to me with a concerned look etched on his face.

"Stay right here, Hannah. Don't move," he ordered.

I felt my own moment of panic as I realized that I couldn't promise that I'd be able to stay right here. I had no idea if, when, or how I'd get back to my own time. Wayne had so far been much too excited to ask any questions, but I wouldn't be able to give him any information about me anyway. It would be disastrous if I disappeared only to have Wayne or Seth find the younger me of this current time, before I'd even originally met Seth.

If Seth arrived tonight, I could talk to him and explain. Then, if I disappeared again, he would understand and wouldn't continue looking for me. Then, maybe, just maybe,

Sicily would be wrong and Seth wouldn't fall back into Katherine's arms. But, if I disappeared before Seth arrived, he would again be left with nothing but a desperate Katherine in need of his love and support. Seth's voice in the car on the day he said goodbye kept running through my head, "If I had only known…"

Wayne hadn't bothered waiting for my promise to stay put. He was sprinting for the door to the lounge.

"Wayne, wait!" I called.

He turned around with obvious impatience.

I hurried to explain. "Please don't ask me any questions. I can't answer them. But, if something happens and I'm not here when Seth arrives, would you please give him this for me?"

Quickly scribbling a note on one of my doodled napkins, I walked over and handed it to him.

After my strange request, Wayne seemed torn, obviously desperate to make his phone call but reluctant to leave me.

"It's okay," I assured. "Go make your call. I'll wait right there on the couch."

With a grin and a promise of, "I'll be quick," he was gone.

Weary from the day's steady emotional turmoil, I flopped down on the couch in front of the fire.

As I sat watching the flames, my mind reviewed the day's bizarre events and ended with one thought: Seth is coming. Comfort washed over me. Everything was going to be okay. He would know what to do. As soon as he arrived,

I'd tell him everything. He was smart. Maybe he'd have an idea about how I was supposed to get back to my own time.

As the mesmerizing flames continued their hypnotic dance, warmth eased my tense muscles. My whole body relaxed. Everything would be fine once Seth was here. He would hold me and…

"She's here! I found her!" I recognized Seth's voice yelling, waking me from my delicious dreams. He had arrived! I felt his hands on my face as I struggled to consciousness.

"Hannah! Hannah, are you okay?" I heard his words, but my brain was not functioning right. I knew I needed to explain. That I needed his help. But it felt like my mouth was full of cotton swabs, and I couldn't form the words.

Suddenly, I was aware of someone else kneeling next to Seth by the couch. She was sobbing and rambling words that I couldn't keep up with.

"Hannah, I'm so sorry! I thought you were gone. I didn't know if you had left or something happened. I shouldn't have fought with you. I thought you had left because you were mad at me, but then you were gone so long and your car was still here. We were so worried. We looked everywhere. I'm so sorry, Hannah!"

It was Abby. I recognized her voice and I remembered our argument, but if Abby was here, then that must mean I was back in my own time. But that couldn't be right because Seth was right beside her, stroking my hair and looking at me with such concern.

"I don't understand," I mumbled. Gathering my thoughts, I asked Abby slowly, "When did we argue about

Dad, Abby?"

"This morning. Don't you remember? Dad's here now. He and some others are searching outside for you. They're due back in a few minutes to check in. I'd better run and tell them we found you." Not waiting for a response, Abby dashed off.

I sighed and closed my eyes. "Then I'm back."

"What do you mean, Hannah?" Seth questioned. "Where have you been all day?"

"It happened again. I went back in time."

Realizing again that things didn't seem quite right in this time frame, I sat up abruptly. Unbelievable pain shot through my head. Responding to my moans, Seth gently pushed me back down on the couch, but the pain didn't ease its grip. If anything, it was only intensifying.

"What is it, Hannah?"

Needing answers, I struggled to push through the pain. "What are you doing here, Seth?"

"You invited me to come spend the holidays with you here at the lodge, remember? I drove up today after my shift at the hospital. You were gone, and we've been frantic searching for you."

"I remember inviting you," I gritted out, "but you were spending the holidays with your fiancé and her family."

"My fiancé? We'd better get you to the hospital for an MRI, Hannah. You obviously have an excruciating headache and you're starting to sound delusional."

"Your fiancé, Seth!" I said fiercely. "You know,

Katherine Colson!"

"Hannah, I have no fiancé! Certainly not Katherine Colson. I haven't even seen Katherine in well over a year, though I do think Wayne said they were back on again in their bipolar relationship."

Now the headache was joined by intense waves of nausea. Moaning and covering my eyes, I persisted. "I don't understand. You and Katherine were engaged."

"Hannah," Seth said patiently. "I have never been engaged to Katherine or anyone else. Why would I want to? We discussed all of this a couple days ago after you showed up at the hospital."

Standing and reaching in his back pocket for his wallet, he pulled something out. It was wrinkled but encased in a plastic covering obviously meant to protect it.

Handing it to me, Seth said, "Don't you remember this? Why would I waste my time with someone else when I knew that somehow, someday you would show up in my life again."

Straining my eyes in the pain-laced light, I saw the napkin I had written on seemingly minutes before. Except now, I realized those minutes were three years ago. Still visible among the doodled flowers on the well-worn napkin, my own handwriting clearly scrawled, "Seth, wait for me. Love, Hannah"

Tears streamed down my face from both emotion and pain. I handed the napkin back to Seth and tried to force myself up off the couch.

"Restroom!" I announced not-so-romantically as I held

my hand over my mouth and prayed I'd make it.

But the second I stood to my feet, I knew I'd made a mistake. I never made it to the restroom. I passed out instead.

CHAPTER NINE

I woke in what should have been the best place on Earth — Seth's arms. Unfortunately, the frantic repetition of my name and hands fluttering around repeatedly checking my vitals was not the least bit romantic. The fact that it still felt like a sharp spike was being drilled slowly into my skull was also a mood killer.

As I worked to control the pain and nausea enough to respond to Seth's questions, Abby, Tom, and my dad rushed into the room.

Breathing a "Thank God," Dad knelt beside me, smoothing the hair back from my face.

"Is she okay?" Dad questioned Seth, who was still holding me securely in his lap.

Eyes closed against the painful glare of the lights, I still managed to intercept Seth's answer. "I'm fine," I gritted out, trying to ease the worry in my dad's voice.

"She is not fine," Seth corrected. "She just passed out. She has an intense headache, dizziness, and nausea. We need to get her to a hospital for an MRI or CT scan, maybe both."

"I'm not going to a hospital!" I argued through clenched teeth. "Just give me a minute and I'll be fine."

"What caused this?" Dad said, ignoring me and focusing on Seth. "Where has she been all day?"

Trying to open my eyes and rouse myself enough to plead my own case, I saw Seth grimace as he answered Dad. "She had another time traveling experience. She mentioned a headache after the first one, but this reaction is far worse."

I felt the tension like electricity from my dad's body as his shock and concern jumped about 10 times. "I'll go get the car," Dad said, rising quickly from his position beside me.

"I am not going to the hospital!" I said fiercely, eyes wide open now. "Stop talking about me like I'm not here! I survived the first time this happened, and I'll survive this one."

"You need to go to the hospital, Hannah." Seth stated firmly. "We don't know what happened, why it happened, or what it did to your brain and your body. I need to run some tests to make sure you're alright."

I purposely elbowed Seth as I tried to wiggle out of his arms. But I couldn't make it off the couch or force him to release his grip on me. "Just give me something for the pain and leave me alone!"

"Hannah-girl, Seth's right, we have to make sure you're okay," Dad said gently.

"No, Hannah's right," Abby announced firmly. I didn't know if she was still feeling bad over our earlier argument or if she actually thought I was right, but I didn't really care. I was just ready to pin a medal on my wonderful, loyal big sister.

"Think about it," Abby continued. "This reaction is obviously worse than her first one, but, like she said, she recovered. We can't just waltz into an ER claiming that she is having side effects from time travel. They will immediately order a psych evaluation on her and maybe the rest of us as well. If by chance someone actually believes us or finds something irregular in her tests, they will want to lock her up for study."

"But that's exactly why she should go to the hospital." Tom inserted. "We need to find out what's happening, no matter what it takes. This could continue happening, with a worse reaction next time. Not to mention the effect she's surely having on the timeline. Right now these experiences are dangerous to both Hannah and others. They need to be stopped."

Glaring at Tom, Abby argued vehemently, "I'm not ready to see Hannah put through a bunch of tests and medications to figure out something that no one understands or even has experience with. Just give her a little time. If she isn't better by tomorrow, you can always take her to the hospital then."

I finally relaxed and tried to breathe deeply through the pain. Abby was fully capable of fighting my battles. I knew I would not be going anywhere tonight.

Looking up into Seth's eyes, I saw he was torn between the desire to get me some help and the fear that help might actually harm me.

"Okay, Abby," Seth said slowly. "It's up to your dad for the final say, but I'm fine with waiting. I agree that I'm not sure it's a good idea to involve other people right now. I can give Hannah something to make her more comfortable and watch her through the night. If she's not better tomorrow, we'll have to take her in."

After a long searching look that creased worry lines in his brow, Dad nodded and said, "Abby, go get Hannah's bed ready. What do you need, Seth?"

Once again, Seth carried me gently up the stairs of the lodge. The motion made the dizziness and nausea worse. Thankfully, Abby, had a bucket waiting when we got to my room. To my utter embarrassment, I made full use of the bucket while Seth held my hair back. While Seth left to get his bag, Abby helped me dress in my pajamas and get in bed.

Seth returned equipped with a well-stocked medical bag. "I had no idea that doctors nowadays traveled with a fully stocked pharmacy for house calls," I remarked.

Seth smiled, "They don't, but thankfully your doctor isn't a regular one. I carry this with me because I do sometimes make house calls for patients who have been recently released from the hospital. Because I'm involved with a lot of experimental treatments, I have to closely monitor those patients involved in the studies."

"You won't get in trouble for using some of the medication on me?" I asked weakly, remembering only too well the recent fiasco over medication missing from a hospital.

"Not at all. I just have to keep a log of everything I use. I can't guarantee that you won't receive a bill, though," he said with a grin. "The hospital tends to be pretty picky about being reimbursed."

"I've actually made use of this medical bag quite frequently." Seth continued as he checked my blood pressure and other vitals for the umpteenth time. "My superiors find it rather amusing the way medical emergencies seem to find me. Their current favorite happened when I was at a zoo with some friends. A lady tripped over a loose peacock and got a nasty gash on her arm. It was bleeding heavily, so I just took care of it there with my medical bag. Unfortunately, I didn't have anything in my bag to help Mr. Peacock with his nasty limp."

I giggled and moaned at the same time. "Seth, please stop!" I pleaded. "It hurts my head to laugh."

"Sorry, I guess I'll just have to save the other stories for later. The one about the cheerleaders is really good too, but not as funny as the one about the sea lion."

Seth was concerned that I wouldn't be able to keep down any pills, but I couldn't handle the thought of baring my rear for him to give me an injection. If he just wasn't so handsome and charming, I could've done it. Instead, I made him give me a couple pills, which I prayed would not be making a return trip.

The medication worked quickly. I felt myself become drowsy even as I tried to focus on what Seth was saying.

"I'm guessing you went back to Christmas three years ago," he said, holding my hand and still looking at me with concerned eyes.

Nodding, I wanted to ask him how he knew, but I couldn't seem to make my mouth form the words. Losing the battle to stay awake, I drifted into a deep, dreamless sleep.

Unfortunately, my sleep wasn't very rejuvenating. It is very difficult to get any quality sleep when somebody wakes you every couple hours to check your vitals and shine a bright light in your eyes. I guess it was sweet that Seth slept on an air mattress beside my bed so he could watch and take care of me. I guess it was touching that he was so concerned that he wanted to check and make sure I didn't have any traumatic brain injury that would send me into a coma. But, by the third wake-up call, I was ready to get violent.

Flailing my arms and slapping away the hands that were trying to wake me, I grabbed the covers and pulled them tightly over my head for protection.

"Leave me alone, Seth!" I grumbled loudly.

"I need to check and make sure you're okay, Hannah," he insisted, trying to peel away my cocoon.

"Seth, the only thing ailing me is the fact that some insane, over-protective doctor keeps waking me up!"

"How's the headache and nausea?"

"A lot better when I'm asleep!" I snapped. "You gave me another dose of medication on your last round of torture. Trust me, I'll let you know if I need anything else. Now, let me sleep!"

"Well, making my assessment based on your mood, vocabulary, and smarty-pants remarks, I would say you're safe to go back to sleep. If those grouchy symptoms continue in the morning, though, I will definitely have to resort to other methods of torture."

After turning off the light, Seth flopped back on his air

mattress. I realized I'd been rude to a wonderful man who was only trying to help me. But, before my feelings of guilt could formulate into an apology, sleep had overtaken me again.

Waking in the morning to sunlight streaming through the window, I found Seth keeping vigil on a chair beside my bed. His fingers were clicking over the keyboard of a laptop.

Remembering my last thoughts before I'd fallen asleep, I spoke quietly, my voice scratchy with the remnants of sleep. "Seth, I'm sorry for being so grouchy. You were only trying to help, and I was mean."

"You're awake!" Seth said, looking up from his work with a smile. "Don't worry about being grouchy. After what you'd been through, you were probably entitled. And I may have slightly overdone the medical monitoring. I was just worried about you. How are you feeling now?"

"Better," I said, taking quick inventory of all my aches and pains. "I still have a headache, but it isn't nearly as severe. I feel really weak, though."

"This might help bring back your strength." With a flourish, he lifted the lid on a tray sitting on the nightstand. A huge, gooey cinnamon roll graced the center of a plate with several strips of crisp bacon attending on the side. Just the sight of the yummy creation made my mouth water.

"I see Abby is still feeling guilty over our argument yesterday." I said, eagerly reaching for the plate. "Grandma's cinnamon rolls are a lot of work."

"I think she woke up early to make sure they were ready for you," Seth explained. "You'll have to be sure to talk to her and relieve her guilt."

Biting into the sugary, delicious piece of heaven, I closed my eyes. "I don't know about that. Right now, I'm thinking I need to make Abby feel guilty more often." With a wide-eyed innocent look that didn't fool Seth at all, I continued, "I wonder how long I can milk this thing. Do you know if she has any of my favorites planned for lunch?"

"Hannah, you're awful!" Seth said with mock horror. "I wouldn't push my luck if I were you. Your sister seems pretty smart. She may feel guilty now, but it probably won't take long to sink in that she really had nothing to do with your disappearance. You'd better enjoy that cinnamon roll. It may be the only peace offering you get."

"Speaking of my disappearance..." I said, turning serious as I remembered his question from last night. "How did you know I went back to Christmas three years ago?"

"It was partially a guess," Seth explained. "When we talked after you found me at the hospital a couple days ago, you spoke in detail about the first time we met, five years ago. You said that you had just returned from that trip through time, and you never mentioned going back to Christmas three years ago. I figured I'd better not say anything about it. I didn't want to mess things up since you obviously didn't know you would go back. That's why I was so concerned about the physical side effects of time traveling again, though. I knew you would."

Seeing the confused look on my face, Seth reached out his hand, caressed my cheek and asked, "Do you not remember anything about that conversation? Don't you remember how excited I was to see my Hannah? How we stayed up half the night just talking and laughing?"

"That's what's confusing me," I tried to explain. "I do remember. I remember what you're talking about, but I also remember what happened originally. As of yesterday morning, in the original timeline that I experienced, you were engaged to Katherine and said you never wanted to see me again."

My mind tried to make sense out of two sets of vivid memories from the past few days. One set was the original one that I experienced where Seth and I had a very bittersweet reunion. Seth was engaged to Katherine, and after going with me to meet the Lawsons, he said a very painful goodbye.

The other set of memories was one that I knew I personally never experienced, but it was implanted in my brain with such clarity there was no difference than if I had. This reunion with Seth was all sweet. He had held me, picked me up and twirled me around, and expressed his joy and excitement freely. We had talked and made plans with no barriers between us. We had met the Lawsons and then arranged to spend Christmas together with my family at Silver Springs after he finished his shift at the hospital the next day.

I clearly remembered each conversation from this new timeline, each emotion, each touch of Seth's hand. My heart thumped with excitement as I relived each event, the memories growing even stronger. Then, in the midst of this newfound joy of wonderful memories and a budding relationship I had only dreamed of, I had an awful realization.

"I changed it," I said, staring dejectedly at nothing in particular. "Tom was right. I changed the timeline from the original, from what it was supposed to be, to something else."

Moaning and rubbing my aching temples, I explained, "I

have new memories, Seth. I remember everything you do, but I also remember the original and how I changed it."

Gathering me in his arms, Seth rubbed my back. "Hannah, it's okay. Remember what you said about the first time you went back and saved the Lawson family? You said that maybe God sent you to that specific time and place. Maybe it's the same this time."

"No, it's not the same," I moaned, feeling my headache intensify and my nausea return. "Is that bucket from last night still around here?"

"Hannah, look at me," Seth commanded firmly. "You can't do anything right now about changing the past, or apparently in your case, the future. You have to relax and let it go. If you don't, you're going to make yourself worse again, and then your dad will really insist that you go to the hospital. Now take a deep breath. Everything is going to be okay."

Seeing me focus and relent at the mention of the hospital, Seth felt safe in continuing to outline a plan. "We will discuss this as much as you want when you're fully recovered. Right now, I'm going to leave while you get a shower. I'll send Abby up to help you get ready. It is Christmas Eve, after all, and we have a lot of celebrating to do."

Standing, he added as an afterthought, "I'll even send her with another cinnamon roll. That might brighten your perspective."

"Seth," I called as he reached the door. "Can you answer one question? Does it happen again? Do you know if I go back a third time?"

Seth looked at me sadly, his forehead creased with

worry. "I don't know, Hannah. I don't think I would know right now, even if you do go back again. From what you've told me, it sounds like history doesn't change until after you go back and do something to change it. In your original timeline, I probably knew nothing about Christmas three years ago because you hadn't gone back yet. Like you, I won't have any memories involving an alteration in this timeline until you go back in time and alter it."

"This is all so confusing!"

"Relax, Hannah. We'll have plenty of time after you recover to figure things out."

Seth left, and I obediently took a shower, scalding hot just the way I like it. Abby was waiting on my bed when I was finished. After she handed me the promised pastry with a rather pitiful and tentative smile, I decided to take the high road and try to alleviate her guilt-ridden misery.

"Abby, you know none of this is your fault," I said. "Nothing you said or did yesterday caused me to go back in time, and I'm pretty sure our fight wasn't big enough to tear a hole in the space-time continuum."

"Don't joke, Hannah," Abby scolded. "You really have no idea what sent you back in time. Maybe it was our argument or something I said."

"That's ridiculous, Abby. If that was true, I would have gone back in time thousands of times before. It's not like this was the first argument we ever had, and I'm sure it won't be our last. You didn't say some magic words and poof, I was gone. You can't walk on eggshells around me, although I actually might appreciate you being a little more agreeable at times."

"So then, what's your theory of why or how you were

sent back?"

"I have no idea. The first time, I thought maybe it was a one-time bizarre assignment from God, but this time, I didn't accomplish anything major. Nothing about this time seemed the same as the first — not in the way I went back or what I accomplished when I was there. I didn't save anyone's life. I don't know why it happened or what caused it to happen. Maybe it was invisible cosmic gases colliding and creating a window in time located in your dining room that I just happened to walk through."

Ignoring my attempt to be lighthearted, Abby went straight for the idea that currently was enough to give me cold sweats if I thought about it too much. "But if you don't know what caused it or why, then that means it might happen again."

Not wanting her to know how terrified that prospect made me, I again focused on being superficial. "Well then, I guess it might not hurt if you were a little nicer to me. Not fighting with you would probably be beneficial to our health in general. You just have to determine right now that I am and always will be right."

"That's not going to happen," Abby said with a slight smile. "If you just weren't wrong so often, I wouldn't feel the need to tell you about it."

We continued to banter back and forth as Abby helped me with my clothes and hair. I was relieved to see the worry and tension leave her face as she slowly seemed to relax. She didn't mention anything more about me going back in time. She didn't ask any more questions. In fact, nobody did.

For the next two days, there seemed to be a moratorium on any mention of my recent experiences. I wondered if Seth had advised everyone to stay away from the subject when he saw how upset and ill it made me after that initial conversation. The other possibility was that everyone was taking a healthy dose of denial for the sake of Christmas.

Everyone did try to pamper me and keep an extra close eye on everything I did as I recovered completely over the next couple days. The only time I was ever left alone in a room was at night when I slept. Even then, I woke up several times to Seth or one of my family members trying to quietly peek in the dark room and make sure I hadn't disappeared again.

Despite the rough prelude, it was a really good Christmas. Seth fit into my family perfectly, like he'd always belonged. Grandma was spending Christmas with my aunt's family and hadn't met Seth yet, but I was sure she would love him as everyone else seemed to.

Even my over-protective dad accepted Seth and showed him a grudging respect. My dad was not the type to be impressed that Seth was a doctor. Occupation didn't matter; he cared about a man's character. When I asked him what he thought of Seth, he said that he was proud of me for picking what seemed to be a decent guy. He said that so far he really appreciated the way Seth McAllister was treating his little girl.

Abby was almost giddy with delight. Her eyes sparkled as she watched the two of us together. She sent me knowing looks every time Seth did something especially thoughtful or sweet, which was quite often. She practically started drooling when Seth took out his guitar and led everyone in singing Christmas carols around the tree on Christmas Eve. Abby had always had a thing for musicians, and Seth's clear baritone was enough to make any woman's heart melt.

And those were just the parts Abby knew about. We didn't really have much chance to speak privately, or I would have told her about the whispered conversations and laughter Seth and I shared as we got to know each other. She would have almost swooned had she known that after the family caroling session Christmas Eve, Seth and I had stayed up and cuddled on the couch in front of the fire. He got out his guitar again and softly sang love songs just for me. The mellow, soothing sound of his voice actually sang me to sleep. He had to wake me up so I could brush my teeth and make it to my own bed.

The only bad thing was that I felt terrible Christmas morning when I didn't have a gift for Seth. I had only actually met Seth four days ago, and everything since then had been a whirlwind. I hadn't exactly had a chance to go shopping for this special man I didn't know existed a week ago.

Everyone else exchanged gifts. Abby and I had our own little book exchange. I got her a new series of books and she got me a different one. Of course, any gift exchanged between Abby and me was always given with the provision that the giver still retained rights to share the item when necessary. With this communal property philosophy, a gift for Abby was really a gift for myself as well. I knew Abby felt the same way. Sharing was one thing we were good at.

Dad loved the picture of a mountain stream I had painted for him, saying that he was going to put it up in his office and brag to everyone about his talented daughter. Seth studied the painting for a long moment as well, clearly appreciating my work. I so wished I'd had time to paint him something as well!

Dad and Grandma went together and got me the purse

I'd been ogling last time Grandma and I went shopping together. It wasn't at all surprising that Grandma picked out Dad's Christmas gifts. My dad hadn't personally chosen a present for Abby or me since we stopped requesting toys. It wasn't that he didn't care; he just wanted to get us something we liked and didn't feel qualified to do so. He usually depended on Grandma or one of his daughters when choosing a gift for the other daughter.

After the gifts were exchanged, Seth and I were left alone in the lounge. Tom had gone to show Dad something new on his computer, and Abby had left to start on the feast she had planned for lunch. I already felt terrible about not having a gift for Seth, and I felt even worse when he sat down beside me and slipped two small packages into my lap. I almost started crying before I even opened them.

"Seth, I feel awful! I didn't get you a gift! I never got a chance. You haven't had a single gift to open this morning."

"Don't feel bad, Hannah. I got a ton of gifts when I saw my parents last weekend. They're having Christmas with my sister, so we celebrated early."

"But when did you get a chance to shop for me? We only decided to spend Christmas together the day before yesterday."

Seth smiled secretively and ducked his head a little self-consciously. "Hannah, I've had plenty of time to shop. For me, we met five years ago, and I've known for three of those years that you would be coming back into my life at some point. I just didn't know when. Buying something for you always seemed to strengthen my faith that you really would come back. Honestly, I probably have stockpiled enough Christmas presents for you to last the next ten years!"

Touched, I finally opened the smaller of the two gifts. It was a beautiful, delicate silver charm bracelet. It had only one charm on it. Examining the tiny charm that was shaped like a bell, I saw that it was engraved. It had the letters S and H along with a date I instantly recognized.

Momentarily speechless at such a sweet and thoughtful gift, Seth carefully clasped the bracelet onto my wrist and hurried to explain, as if he were afraid I didn't like it.

"It's engraved with our initials and the date of when we first met five years ago. I thought I could get you some other charms to go on the bracelet later. You know, charms that could symbolize other things we do together. I already know I'm going to order you another charm engraved with the date of when you came back in my life." He paused and looked at me worriedly. "Do you like it? I can get you something else if you don't."

I looked at him with tears streaming down my face. "I love it, Seth. It's perfect. I don't think I've ever been given such a romantic, thoughtful gift. Thank you. I just wish I had something to give you."

"Hannah, you already gave me the best Christmas present I could ever receive. It just arrived two days early — you. You are all I've wanted for the past five Christmases."

Looking deep into his eyes, it felt like a magnet was drawing us together. Gently, Seth caressed away the tears on my face. Watching his gaze flicker to my lips, I knew he was going to kiss me. My heart accelerated, and the longing I felt for him was almost a physical ache. He slowly, tenderly bent his head…

"Hannah!" Abby yelled, sticking her head in the door of

the lounge as Seth and I jumped apart about two feet. Abby would have kicked herself had she known what she'd interrupted.

"There you are, Hannah," she said, blissfully unaware. "Do you feel up to giving me a hand when you get a chance? You could mash potatoes or shape the rolls — nothing too complicated, I promise."

"Sure," I responded, my voice sounding remarkably normal. "I'll be there in just a couple minutes."

Abby left, and I took a deep breath, turning my attention to the other package I still held. I purposely avoided looking at Seth, trying to ignore the rosy hue my cheeks were turning and the gleam of mischievous amusement I would surely find in Seth's eyes.

Ripping the paper with unnecessary force, I was surprised when a package of napkins and a pen plopped onto my lap. Seeing that the napkins and pens were both high quality, I suddenly understood and laughed.

"For my framed napkin display in my future art gallery?" I questioned, remembering our conversation at the diner when Seth had admired my doodling.

"Well, you do seem to have an interesting compulsion to make napkin art. Wayne even remarked on your strange habit three years ago." Taking out a small box I hadn't noticed, Seth opened it and produced several doodled napkins that I recognized from that night three years ago, each encased in a plastic cover.

"Here I thought you only had the one I wrote the message on," I said, examining Seth's treasure with a smile. "Wait a minute! This isn't one I doodled three years ago. Seth! You swiped the one from the diner the other night too?"

As I studied Seth's handsome face and sheepish grin, I felt a new wave of dizziness, but this one had nothing to do with time travel.

CHAPTER TEN

THE physical effects from my time travel gradually subsided. By the evening of the 26th, the headache, dizziness, and weakness were gone. I felt almost completely normal and couldn't stand the questions in my head any longer.

Not finding Seth in the lodge, I went outside and followed the sound of chopping wood. Seth was by the barn hefting an ax over his head as he split wood for the fireplace. The muted winter sun glistened off the waves and curls in Seth's dark blond hair. The heavy red plaid shirt he wore protected him from the cold, but didn't completely disguise the muscles underneath. I watched as he raised the ax above his head and brought it down quickly, easily splitting the stick of wood before positioning another and repeating the process. The motion seemed almost effortless. His appearance and strength were the epitome of masculinity.

While I tried to control any obvious drooling, Seth looked up to see me watching him. He grinned, set down the ax, and wiped his brow with his sleeve.

"I'm glad to see you, Hannah. You are just the excuse I need to take a break."

"I'm sure Tom and Abby will appreciate you splitting the wood, but they don't expect it. Don't kill yourself doing it." Despite my words, I kind of wished he'd continue his work. I'd been enjoying myself.

"I want to try to earn my keep in some way. Especially since they won't let me pay for my stay. Besides, chopping wood is great exercise."

Several decorative benches were placed for guests around the grounds of Silver Springs. As Seth and I sat on one together, I came right to the point.

"I'm completely recovered now, Seth. I'm ready to talk. I need to talk," sounding stilted in my anguish even to my own ears, I pressed on. "I feel like I've made a mess of things. Tom was right. I've changed history and I had no business doing so."

"It's not like you could've helped it, Hannah. You didn't choose to go back in time, and, given the circumstances, I'm sure you did what you felt was right."

"That's partially true," I said. Painstakingly, I told him the details of what had happened three years ago. How I used my future knowledge to figure out what was really going on with Wayne and the drugs and then how I talked him out of taking the blame.

"Hannah, none of what you told me was bad for you to do. You made sure that the truth came out. That was beneficial for all involved."

"But that's not all I did," I said, and with misery in my eyes, I explained how Natalie had said that she thought Katherine and Seth would probably get back together because he'd want to help her. I already knew they were engaged in the original timeline. But I'd wanted Seth for myself. I'd selfishly sent Seth the note to wait for me, knowing that it could potentially alter the future. "You see, Seth. I didn't save a bunch of lives. I didn't prevent a great travesty. It was me, not God. I was selfish, and I changed the way things were supposed to be because I didn't like the outcome."

"But you are assuming the timeline you first experienced was the right one. How do you know you weren't supposed to go back and change it?"

"I might be able to buy that if I had done something noble, but I didn't. In some ways, I knew what I was doing, and I did it anyway. I wanted you to be with me instead of Katherine." Avoiding looking directly at Seth, I carefully studied my fingernails that were desperately in need of a manicure. It was so embarrassing to admit my feelings for Seth and to confess what I had done to get my own way.

Seth was quiet for a minute, and then, interrupting my fingernail inspection, he asked softly, "After we met again in your original timeline, did I still want to be engaged to Katherine? Did I not have feelings for you? Because I can't imagine being able to shut those off."

I felt myself blush to the roots of my hair. "You said you had feelings for me, but you insisted on remaining loyal and keeping your commitment to Katherine. You said if you'd only known that I was coming back, things might have been different. That's what gave me the idea to send you the note in the first place."

"Then you shouldn't feel bad about changing history, Hannah. You were able to help everyone get what they wanted. I imagine that in that first timeline, I would've gone ahead and married Katherine, but I don't think I could have been happy knowing that you were still out there and I had missed my chance."

Seeing that I still wasn't convinced, Seth continued. "I don't really know the ethics of time travel, but I still maintain that maybe you were meant to go back and change history and that the current timeline is the right one."

"How can you feel that way?" I questioned, too scared to latch onto the hope he was offering. "Tom seemed to be pretty adamant that I shouldn't have changed history in any way."

"I like Tom, but he doesn't strike me as a very spiritual person. I try not to underestimate God. I've always imagined my God had the foreknowledge of how I was going to mess up and was big enough to handle turning my faults into something good."

"So, you're saying that maybe I was meant to travel back and change time, almost predestined. That God knew I would be selfish and could use even my faults to achieve His result."

"Exactly right."

Biting my lip in thought, I replied, "I don't know that I can buy that. I got what I wanted, but I did it at the expense of another. I got you, but because of my actions, Katherine got kicked out of medical school and lost you as well."

"No, Hannah, you created a better future for everyone, including Katherine. Katherine did have to leave medical school, but only a small number of people know the truth about it. Her parents are quite wealthy and influential, and they were able to sweep the circumstances under the carpet. According to everyone else, Katherine took a break from an extremely stressful year of medical school to vacation at an exclusive spa. Of course, it was actually a celebrity rehab facility. According to the press release, though, Katherine came home from the spa with a better outlook on life and a clearer understanding of what she wanted. She decided not to return to medical school, but enrolled in law school instead. As difficult as she found medical school, she thrived in law school. She is now a very accomplished attorney who specializes in medical law.

"Wow! I had no idea!" I said, shocked. "Katherine was a nurse in the first timeline. What about Wayne? Is he okay?"

"I don't know what happened to Wayne originally, but now he couldn't be better. He is finishing his residency, like me. He is already a very gifted and highly respected research doctor. He did his residency at a very prominent hospital across the country and even went overseas several times to study and contribute to research. He already has several amazing offers to continue specializing in research after his residency, but the man has already had tremendous impact in the field of medicine."

"That's such a relief! Originally, Wayne was a used car salesman."

Seth laughed. "Well, that lets you know that your original timeline was completely wrong. Wayne could be a used car salesman like I could train wild animals for a circus!"

"Are you two still friends?"

"Best friends. In fact, I called him a couple of days ago and told him that you'd finally shown up again. I explained about the whole time travel thing, and he actually believed me. It's a miracle in itself to have literal, scientific Wayne believe something so seemingly far-fetched as time travel. I guess having experienced something of it firsthand, he couldn't deny it was the only explanation that made sense."

At my questioning look, Seth continued, "Wayne took it pretty hard three years ago when he went back in the lounge and found you'd disappeared. He turned all of Silver Springs upside down looking for you and was a basket-case when I arrived. He blamed himself, saying he never should have left you alone. It wasn't as hard on me because I'd already gone through one of your mysterious disappearances before. Plus, Wayne gave me your note. It was a tremendous relief knowing you were real and I could stop looking for you. You would come back into my life at some point on your own."

"I'm so glad things have worked out so well for both Wayne and Katherine. I still don't know that I can believe that this timeline is now the way things should be." Thinking quietly for a moment, I finally admitted my biggest fear. "I don't think I could handle it if I time traveled again. Not just the physical effects, but emotionally, it would be almost unbearable. I can't handle any more responsibility for changing the course of history. Tom was right, it's too dangerous for myself and the human race in general!"

"On one hand, I think God can handle one little Hannah Kraeger," Seth said, picking up my hand and holding it. "I don't think you would change the course of human events unless He wanted you to. But, on the other hand, I am worried about you going back again. You've traveled twice in only a few days, with increasingly worse side effects. I really think we should go and have a battery of tests done at the hospital. We can make sure you're healthy and see if there are any abnormalities that may be triggering these episodes or any lingering effects."

I made a face. "Let's wait awhile, Seth. As scared as I am about time traveling, I'm more scared right now of somehow being made into a lab rat."

"I'd protect you."

"You're a resident, Seth. You couldn't protect me, especially if someone important finds out that I actually have time traveled. No, let's just wait. Maybe you're right and we are now currently living in the correct timeline, the way things should be. If your theory is true, then I really won't travel again because there isn't anything to fix."

"I appreciate you trying to use my own ideas against me, Hannah, but it's not going to work. You need to have some testing done. My superiors will grant approval, and I can do the tests myself if you'll just let me."

"No, Seth," I said, clenching my jaw and trying not to get aggravated. "I don't want to discuss this right now. Just give me until after New Year's and we can talk about it if you want." I was really just trying to use a stall tactic. I had no intention of having any tests done at any time, but I knew I had to try to at least fake a compromise to appease Seth.

Reading a slight acceptance on Seth's face, followed by a dubious look as if he were questioning my true intentions, I quickly changed the subject. "I seem to remember you saying something a couple of days ago about Wayne and Katherine's bipolar relationship. Does Katherine still resent Wayne for turning her in?"

"No, not at all. Quite the opposite actually. Wayne has always been crazy about her, but she'd never given him the time of day before the drug incident. After that, she actually seemed to respect him and appreciate that he'd gotten her help. Wayne really supported her throughout her treatment, and they've been dating off and on ever since."

"Wow, I didn't really expect that. Wayne was so in love with her three years ago and felt awful for turning her in. Katherine wouldn't even look at him when she left. Why the 'off' in their relationship now? Why not just 'on?'"

"I don't really know for sure. Wayne doesn't really talk about it that much. I do know Katherine can be very hot and cold. She can be a very difficult person to love. When I talked with him the other day, he mentioned he was spending Christmas with Katherine, so I think they're currently back 'on.'"

"Oh," Seth added, almost as an afterthought. "Wayne did say something else, but I didn't really understand it. He wants to come see you in person some time, but he said to tell you that he was ready now to say that thank you. He also said to tell you that he's long overdue for a promised chess rematch. He wanted me to warn you that he's had three years to prepare."

I smiled. I'd still beat him no matter how prepared he was.

"You never told me you played chess," Seth said, a small sliver of hurt in his voice.

I laughed. "There's a lot about me that you don't know! Technically, we only met less than a week ago. It just seems a lot longer."

"Yeah, at least five years."

As we'd been talking, the sun had been nearing the horizon and was just beginning to send color up the sky from the west.

"I need to finish my project before it gets dark," Seth said, standing from the bench and stretching.

Seth went back to chopping wood in the fading light, and I went back to watching him. His movements were fluid, almost graceful. Seth McAllister had to be the sexiest man alive. I could think of only one thing that might make this scene better.

"Isn't it a gorgeous evening?" Seth asked, pausing in his chopping to look around at the tall pines silhouetted against the setting sun. The sky was alive as streaks of pink and orange intermixed with blue to paint a landscape that looked like a watercolor done by a master artist.

"It is nice," I agreed, looking directly at him. "But I think the scenery would be much improved if the temperature was at least fifty degrees warmer."

Seth looked at me, obviously mystified. "What are you talking about? It's December. If it was fifty degrees warmer, we wouldn't have had a white Christmas. The snow would be gone and everything would be drab and muddy."

"True. But if it were warmer, maybe you wouldn't need so many layers as you chopped wood. *My* view would definitely improve." Yes, I thought, a shirtless Seth in the fading glory of sunset would be the only thing that could be sexier.

Now, fully understanding my train of thought, Seth tipped his head back and laughed. "You little minx!"

Even though I was fiercely blushing over my own boldness, I didn't regret sharing my thoughts with Seth. There was something about Seth that made me feel both comfortable and alive. The electricity between us was undeniable, but I also felt that I could be myself around him. Normally very reserved, I had never felt so close to someone in such a short amount of time. I could share anything with him, even thoughts I would normally never breathe to a soul. I had a strange, utter assurance that I would be accepted by Seth no matter what.

Eyes sparkling, Seth set his ax down, walked over, and playfully pulled me up from the bench. As he did, a package fell out of my oversized coat.

"Oh," I said, bending the retrieve the rectangle wrapped in red Rudolf paper. "I almost forgot to give you your present. I'm sorry I didn't have anything for you yesterday. This is nothing special, but it was all I could come up with on short notice."

The gift distracted Seth from whatever playful intentions he'd had.

"Hannah, you shouldn't have!" he said instead, obviously surprised. "On the other hand, I've never refused a present." With a boyish grin, Seth took the gift and removed the paper. For a moment, he was quiet as he stared at the frame.

As he studied the gift, I explained, "You appreciated my napkin art so much, I thought you should get a first edition piece using the napkins you gave me for Christmas. Who knows," I teased, "maybe napkin art will be the next big thing in the world of Art Nouveau. Society just might be ready for that art gallery of mine."

When he still didn't respond, I tried to explain further, thinking he didn't understand the drawing. "Seth, it's you and me on the night we met."

Using a black ink pen, I had sketched two figures sitting

in front of a fire. The man was cradling the woman close, looking into her sad face, and wiping a tear off her cheek. Ink is a very harsh and unforgiving medium, but I thought I had done a decent job of capturing the features and emotion of both Seth's face and my own. I'd completed the gift by putting it in a simple matted frame Abby had found somewhere.

"Hannah, I know what it is," Seth finally responded. "I was just amazed at what a remarkable artist you are. This is a beautiful picture, napkin and all. Thank you. You couldn't have given me a better present."

His blue-green eyes, full of emotion, locked with mine. I couldn't identify the emotion. I didn't know if he was touched by the gift, memories of the night we met, or the current flowing between us. All I knew was that I couldn't look away.

He slowly reached out a hand and caressed my cheek. "I waited so long for you to come back, Hannah. No other woman could even compare. So brave, so talented, so breathtakingly beautiful."

As the first stars peeked through the fading brilliance of the sunset, my eyes traced Seth's features. I could still see his eyes sparkling and the scruffy five-o'clock shadow that only made his strong face more masculine and irresistible.

He tilted my chin up with gentle fingers. Other than the moment Abby had interrupted in the lounge yesterday, Seth had never made an attempt to kiss me. I knew he was attracted to me, our chemistry was unmistakable. But, up till now, he had kept his distance.

As his gaze focused on my lips, I knew now was the moment. He was going to kiss me. I ached for him to kiss me. My heart raced and my breathing grew shallow. I felt a yearning for him, an ache in my chest like I'd run too fast for too long.

Slowly, gently, his hands slid around my back and drew me close. I closed my eyes as our lips came together like two magnets. He held me like his most treasured possession. His lips were gentle and feather light, the passion under the surface, revealing itself as the kiss deepened. It seemed like Seth didn't want to scare me with the depth of his emotion, as if he held back a little. I didn't really think of any of this until later, though, because the moment his lips touched mine, every coherent thought flew out of my head. The only thing I knew was that his kiss was like nothing I'd ever experienced before.

Drawing back, Seth whispered my name and held me close. Not wanting the moment to end, we stood in each other's arms until the cold temperature had erased all feeling from my boot-encased toes. We didn't really say anything more, content to be close and watch the concert in the sky as thousands of stars made their nightly appearance.

Snuggling in his embrace, I realized Seth McAllister was the smartest, sweetest, most thoughtful, best-looking man I'd ever met. And he kissed like Prince Charming and Casanova all rolled into one. All things considered, he was perfect.

CHAPTER ELEVEN

THE man had faults — plenty of them. And over the next few months, I had the privilege of discovering and thoroughly inspecting every single one.

One of Seth's most annoying faults was his stubbornness. Seth preferred the terms "determined," "strong-willed," or "goal-oriented." I just went with "stubborn" coupled with the appropriate descriptive adjectives as the situation warranted.

When he got an idea in his head, he wouldn't ever let it go. I guess that trait had served him well in finishing medical school and becoming a successful doctor at such a young age. However, in a relationship, it was aggravating to say the least.

My New Year's stall-and-forget tactic didn't work. Instead, the stubborn man regularly nagged me about having medical tests done. Even though I went the next five months without even a hint of any more time travel, he still brought up the subject over and over again. There was nothing wrong with me physically, I didn't even get the nasty winter cold everyone at college had the month of February. I simply saw no reason to do testing when there wasn't even a problem, but Seth just wouldn't let it go.

His other particularly annoying fault was his love of surprises. I've never really liked surprises. I'm more of a planner. I appreciate being able to anticipate, prepare, and get used to the idea. Seth liked to be spontaneous. Some of his surprises were sweet and romantic, like showing up in a tux on a weekend I wasn't expecting him and taking me to the current Broadway production lighting up the city. Other surprises were just plain obnoxious. He was even the type of guy whose humor appreciated the old open-a-jar-and-have-something-pop-out-at-you trick.

And, yes, he had been known to use a whoopee cushion on occasion.

Despite his faults, I really didn't have much to complain about. In fact, those months between Christmas and graduation were the happiest I'd ever had in my life.

Seth finished his residency while I finished my undergraduate degree. We lived about an hour and a half apart, and usually saw each other on Seth's day off. He would frequently stay overnight at my dad's house. My dad was now a very active member of the Seth McAllister fan club. I was now a little afraid that if Seth and I ever did have a major argument and break up, my dad might actually side with Seth!

Seth and I agreed early on to take things slowly in our relationship. We knew that we had met under unusual and emotionally charged circumstances, and we didn't want that to be the basis and trademark of our relationship. As Seth

Amanda Tru

said, he wanted more with me than an intense roller coaster ride that crashed and burned. For the most part, we were very successful at taking things slowly. We talked a lot and really got to know each other. He became my best friend. The firework chemistry was still there, but we even managed to dial back the earth-shattering kisses as we tried to build more than just a physical relationship.

Riding in Seth's car with the top down a week before graduation, I felt that life was going almost perfectly for me. I was graduating, and I had the man of my dreams in my life. I still had concerns, but I tried to keep those in the background and enjoy the talks, walks, and adventures of my relationship with Seth. Every so often though, I would still have guilt that I had changed history to suit my own purposes. Not knowing what had caused me to time travel in the first place, I also had a nagging fear that I would one day turn around and find that I had gone back in time again.

Now in route for another one of Seth's numerous surprises, we were driving to a yet undisclosed location. I was in a good mood, and, today being my twenty-fourth birthday, I was willing to give Seth a little latitude in the surprise department. I knew he thoroughly enjoyed planning surprises for me and would have something special planned for my birthday. Resolving to relax and enjoy it despite my strict type-A tendencies and strong aversion to surprises, I smiled over at Seth, squeezed his free hand, and relished the feel of the warm wind whipping through my hair.

My relationship with Seth really couldn't have been better. Neither one of us had ever said the L-word, after all we were taking things slowly. But, I knew I felt it, and I was pretty sure he felt the same. I really couldn't imagine ever feeling for someone else the way I felt for Seth.

Of course, while being whisked away by my Prince Charming to some sort of happily ever after, my overactive brain would still occasionally find some nuggets to worry about. Both Seth and I were still undecided about what we were going to do in this next stage of our lives. Seth had a lot of offers around the country to work and finish training in a specialty, but he hadn't made any decision about which one he'd accept.

I still didn't know what I was going to do after graduation either. Seth had offered to sponsor the start-up capital for an art gallery, but there was no way I was going to let him do that. I had way too much pride, even though Seth apparently had way too much money.

Also concerning to me was the fact that I had never met Seth's parents. His dad had been very successful in international trade, but was now retired. Because of his reputation and strong ties overseas, he was still frequently called upon as a diplomat. I hadn't met them yet because they had been out of the country for the last five months.

Even though Seth was confident that they'd love me, I was still not sure. Seth was a very optimistic person who considered me near perfect. Although he frequently encountered my quirks and problems, he preferred to keep his rose-colored glasses firmly in place when looking at me. Unfortunately, I knew his parents would be far more discriminating. Worse, I knew my own faults were numerous.

As we drove south on the freeway, the warmth of the late afternoon sun on my skin and the heavenly aromas of various spring blossoms were just about worth enduring any surprise Seth had planned. I really had no idea where he was taking me. He'd told me to dress nice but comfortable, so that really didn't give me any clues. Maybe we were going to a nice romantic dinner at a restaurant, a concert, or a picnic and walk on the beach. Some of Seth's surprises the last five months had been a lot of fun, even if I would have preferred to know about the plan prior to the adventure. I had told him to keep my birthday plans simple, so I really didn't think he'd go to the extravagance of a helicopter ride at sunset again. Besides, Seth rarely repeated surprises. He delighted in planning something new that I would never think of.

After driving for well over an hour, Seth exited the freeway in the bayside town of Pacific Grove. He then turned onto a winding road that climbed the cliffs overlooking the ocean. When he turned onto what appeared to be a long private driveway flanked by beautiful shade trees, I wondered if he was taking me to an exclusive restaurant or spa.

The drive opened to reveal a gorgeous house. It was a huge mansion, but not at all ostentatious. Every detail, from the perfect landscaping to the rocker on the front porch, was created with an exquisite, understated taste. It really didn't look like a restaurant or a spa; it looked like someone's home.

"Where are we?" I asked, confused and scanning every shadow for some kind of sign.

Seth stopped the car near the front door, and turned to me almost hesitantly. Taking a deep breath, he said in a rush, "This is my parents' house."

I think he said something else after that, but I honestly didn't hear him. I stared at him as waves of panic and feelings of inferiority threatened to roll over me. Suddenly, I opened the car door, jumped out, and started walking briskly in the opposite direction of the house.

Seth caught up with me before I'd gotten far and swung me around to face him.

"Hannah, did you even hear what I said?"

"Are you going to take me back to my apartment or am I going to walk?"

"Hannah, just wait! Let me explain."

"I am *NOT* meeting your parents like this Seth! It's not fair! Why would you surprise me on my birthday with something like this? What were you thinking?"

"Listen, Hannah, It's not what you think. Not exactly." Cupping my face, Seth made me look him in the eye. He probably needed the physical assurance that I was listening to him. "There are a lot of people in that house, people you know and love, who are waiting to give you a surprise party. Please don't disappoint them."

Seth really knew how to play dirty. He knew I liked to please others and hated to think I had disappointed someone I loved.

"Your parents are there too though, right?" I questioned, concerned that he still wasn't telling me the absolute truth.

"Yes, they are," he said, his eyes still locked with mine in an honest exchange. "This is the house they bought after Dad retired. They wanted to meet you. I know it was rotten for me to do it this way, but I was afraid you would worry yourself sick if we arranged and planned a formal meeting."

"But Seth, look at this place," I said, gesturing to the obvious wealth it took to create such a paradise. "I didn't realize... your parents, you, are in a completely different sphere than I am. You've seen the house I grew up in.

You've seen my apartment and old SUV. Your parents are going to hate me. I obviously don't belong here and can never hope to be good enough for their son. Look at me," I said with tears in my eyes as I gestured to what I felt was a frumpy ensemble on an equally dowdy twenty-four-year-old girl.

"Hannah, I *am* looking at you," Seth responded, as he reached out and enfolded me in his embrace. "You're beautiful, inside and out. You belong with me. My parents will see both those things and love you."

Tipping my chin and giving a feather-light kiss to my lips and nose, Seth smiled. "Now, put that inferiority complex back in the closet so the birthday girl can come enjoy her party."

Knowing there was no graceful way to get out of the situation, I relented and let Seth lead me up the wide steps to the front door. Winking playfully back at me as he knocked on the door, Seth then swung the door open with a flourish to a deafening chorus of "Surprise!"

I pasted on a smile as the faces of friends and family swam in front of my vision, all talking and giving me birthday wishes. Feeling slightly overwhelmed, I was grateful when Seth raised his voice over the roar.

"Why doesn't everyone head out back? I think the patio is loaded with refreshments and we can have Hannah open her presents out there."

At the mention of food, everyone willingly exited the entry area. Looking around, I saw that the inside of the house was equally, if not more impressive, than the outside. I was standing on a marble floor in a wide entryway that stretched forward to meet an impressive marble grand staircase. Looking up, a huge chandelier hung from the high vaulted ceiling, shining light onto the polished marble and the two people looking at me below.

Seth's parents were trim, attractive people. Their appearance actually didn't seem to match their opulent surroundings. Their clothing was too simple, their smiles too genuine and friendly to echo the cold formality of the entryway.

Seth had been at least partially right about one thing. Because this meeting with his parents had been so unexpectedly sprung on me, I hadn't had the chance to feel the overwhelming nerves I would've normally felt. Of course, my normal nervousness might also have been somewhat masked by my residual anger at Seth for plotting to put me in this awkward position.

I knew that Seth had never told his parents the specific details of how we'd met or of my knack for time travel. I figured I had at least a shot of a first impression that was favorable and didn't include questions about my sanity. All considered, I managed to adopt a genuine smile and extend a steady hand as Seth spoke and I walked forward to greet the couple.

"Hannah, I'd like you to meet my parents, John and Julie."

John McAllister looked like an older version of Seth. Both were tall and well-built. John's hair was silver, but I could tell it had once been wavy and dark blond like his son's. Unlike Seth, Julie was very petite and had straight dark hair, but Seth had inherited her blue-green eyes, wide smile, and deep dimple in the right cheek. She was still very pretty with a beautiful complexion even a woman my age could envy.

"I'm glad to finally meet you," I greeted, deliberately trying to be friendly despite my natural reserve.

"So this is the young lady who has turned my son's world upside down," John said with a smile as he grasped my hand in both of his.

"I feel like I already know you," Julie responded, ignoring my offered hand and reaching for a hug instead.

Releasing me, Julie looked closely at my face, her own friendly countenance changing to one of worry. "First off, Hannah, let me apologize for my son's behavior. I was not in favor of him surprising you with meeting us. I didn't think it fair, and I tried to talk him out of doing it."

"Thank you. I appreciate your understanding. Surprises definitely are not my thing. But, I feel like I should also apologize to you as well." At the confused looks on both of their faces, I shot a fierce look in Seth's direction before continuing. "In all honesty, I will be plotting a very serious and nasty revenge against your son."

Seth's parents burst out laughing while Seth tried unsuccessfully to portray looks of hurt and innocence.

"Trust me, Hannah," Julie said, her eyes twinkling brightly, "there is no apology necessary."

"That boy deserves everything you can dish out and more, little girl," John agreed. "He's blessed all of us at one time or another with one of his unpleasant surprises."

Seth piped up, "Not that I would have any reason to change the subject, but we do have a large number of guests out back and a birthday party waiting."

Still laughing, Seth's parents turned to lead the way through the house. Seth pulled me close, placed a kiss above my left ear, and whispered, "You did good, Hannah. Now relax."

I arched my eyebrows and leveled a calculating look at him. "I was serious about getting revenge, Seth."

"I know you were serious, Sweetheart," Seth answered, a teasing light in his eyes. "You are certainly welcome to try."

I narrowed my eyes and glared at him. Seth's cocky attitude made me all the more determined to teach him a lesson. Apparently, I didn't scare him, and, like an excited puppy, he began dragging me through the house.

Sweeping my gaze over the rooms on either side as we went, I guessed that the entryway was the most formal in the entire house. Everything else seemed to have a very homey, understated décor that seemed more fitting John and Julie McAllister.

Exiting some French doors at the end of the kitchen, we stepped out into a beautiful backyard. It was expertly landscaped with lush trees and fragrant flowers chosen and positioned perfectly to highlight a breathtaking view of the ocean below. As the final rays of the sun faded, lights twinkled on in the city lining the shore to the north, creating a beautiful mosaic that reminded me of the Light Bright I had as a child.

There were a lot of people, all visiting and enjoying what looked to be delicious catered finger foods attractively spread on tables. I wasn't a social butterfly by nature, so I was kind of surprised Seth had found this many people to attend my party. My family was there, even a couple of my aunts and cousins who lived in the area. Grandma came right over, hugging me and giving me a quick once-over with her knowing eyes to make sure I had survived the surprise. Several friends from my church and college had come as well.

I was glad to see Natalie and Sicily had made it. I had struck up a good friendship with the two doctors after running into them again at Seth's hospital. They were a lot of fun, and best of all, they had never once asked pointed, intrusive questions about my strange disappearance three years ago. They were apparently content to accept friendship on my terms, and I was very appreciative.

Seeing Abby standing near the barbeque Seth's dad was firing up, I rushed over and hugged my sister.

"I'm glad to see Seth is still living," she said. "I seriously had my doubts after the stunt he pulled getting you here. You don't like surprises; everyone knows that."

"Oh, Seth knows, he just feels he's exempt. His surprises are different," I mocked, rolling my eyes.

"I guess you'll have to forgive him. You just can't hold a grudge against such a hottie."

Looking over to see Seth laughing with some friends, white teeth and dimples flashing, I had to agree. "Yeah," I said, noting the muscled biceps peeking out of his short sleeve polo shirt. "If the guy didn't look like a Greek god, he'd be in serious trouble."

"It is kind of sweet, though." Seeing that I was not overly angry about the surprise, Abby felt safe to shift loyalties. She was, after all, one of Seth's biggest fans. "He did go to a lot of work to make your birthday special."

I know, but it does make me sad that you won't even be around next week for us to celebrate your birthday. Maybe we should have had a combo birthday party like when we were kids."

"No, Hannah, this is your night. Besides, Tom has his own special plans for my birthday. We're just going to be in the Caribbean on vacation for it."

"I'm not even sure why you guys even need a vacation. You live at one of the number one vacation destinations in the state. Why would you even need to leave your own paradise?"

Abby made a face. "I'm not the one who really needs a vacation," she said, looking discreetly over to where Tom was talking with Seth's dad. "Let's just say, Tom's not nearly as enthusiastic about Silver Springs as I am."

"Wow, that's surprising! I thought it was the perfect situation for both of you. You got to run Silver Springs while he got to telecommute. You employ other people to do cleaning and maintenance. You run a successful business. It's like you get to live in a postcard with its own year-round hot springs. What's not to like?"

Abby shrugged. "I guess he misses what he calls 'civilization.'" Taking a deep breath and brightening with noticeable effort, Abby continued. "So, anyway, that's why this vacation is going to be good for us. Bermuda here we come!"

Sensing there was much more to the story than Abby was telling me, I was considering whether or not to push for more information, when an unexpected voice grabbed my attention.

"Hey, stranger!" the familiar voice said. "I've finally come to issue my thank you in person."

"Wayne!" Happily, I gave him a quick hug and pulled back to assess any changes to the man I hadn't technically seen in three years. Being so busy finishing his residency, Wayne hadn't had a chance to come visit until now. "Now this is the kind of surprise I like!"

"You look exactly the same, Hannah. I wonder why that is?" he said teasingly. Wayne looked the same himself, with the possible exception of a few more laugh lines around the eyes. Wayne was the epitome of tall, dark, and handsome.

"Good genetics, I suppose," I teased back. "I age very well."

Turning suddenly serious, Wayne looked around, making sure we weren't being overheard. Abby had moved back over to Tom and was now talking with another couple.

"I do need to thank you, Hannah. You were right about everything. Of course, now I know why you were right, but I still appreciate you having the guts to step in and confront me. I don't know what would have happened if you hadn't been there, but I'm sure grateful you were."

"I'm probably the only person who knows exactly what would have happened if I wasn't there, and trust me, you are better off. That is, unless you have a secret desire and calling on your life to sell used cars."

Wayne looked confused and had just opened his mouth to ask a question when I quickly back-pedaled. "Don't ask.

You don't want to know. Just be grateful that I probably broke all the ethics of time travel and changed history. You, at least, are much better off."

Looking around at all the guests, I asked, "Where's Katherine? Isn't she here with you?"

"No." Pausing noticeably, as if trying to think of an appropriate explanation, Wayne finally shrugged and finished simply, "She couldn't make it."

"Ah," I said, reading between the lines, "So she still hates me."

"There you go again, Hannah, being so blamed intuitive." Sighing and running a hand through his hair, he admitted. "Yeah, she hates you. I don't know why, but she certainly does."

"I could tell she hated me when she glared at me as she was leaving the lodge three years ago," I said, involuntarily shivering at the memory of the look in her eyes. "I don't know how, but she seemed to know that I had something to do with your change of heart. Did you ever tell her that I talked you out of taking the blame?"

"No, I've never told her anything about you. I don't know how she would know, if she even does. I don't know that is the reason for her dislike. She certainly bears no hard feelings toward me over the incident. I think it might have just been that she hated you the first time she laid eyes on you."

"That sounds a bit psychotic."

"That's just Katherine," Wayne explained with a sad little smile. "I don't understand her. I can't seem to live with her, but I can't seem to live without her." He shrugged helplessly, and I remembered what Seth had said about Katherine being a difficult person to love.

"Hey, everybody! Come and get it!" Seth called loudly. "Supper's ready! We'll let Hannah open her gifts afterwards.

As everyone moved toward the tables and the delicious aroma of barbequed steaks, Wayne leaned over and whispered, "You still owe me a chess game. Tonight. And I won't feel the least bit bad about beating the birthday girl."

Dinner was fantastic. Along with the steaks, there were baked potatoes, green salads, fresh fruit salads, hot biscuits, and a couple of dishes I didn't recognize but tasted delicious. Conversation around the table was lively, and I thoroughly enjoyed myself. At one point, Seth grabbed and squeezed my hand under the table. Then he looked at me as if to say, "See I told you this was a good surprise."

Then, as if suddenly remembering, he said, "Matt and Kelly wanted me to wish you a Happy Birthday for them as well. They were planning on coming tonight, but the baby got sick."

"Oh, I hope she's okay," I said, concerned.

"She should be fine," Seth replied. "They think she just has a stomach bug."

After dinner, I was made to sit in a "seat of honor," and given numerous presents to unwrap. The gifts were overwhelming and ranged from the humorous to the touching. Never in my life had I received so many gifts. Books, clothes, movies, and other items began piling up on the table next to me. Abby and Tom gave me some clothes. I always appreciated when Abby bought me clothes because her taste always seemed far superior to mine.

Grandma gave me a beautiful quilt she had made herself. Standing and spreading it open to show off the design, a paper fell to the ground. Stooping to retrieve it, I saw that it said: "For my Hannah. Every girl needs something for her hope chest. Love, Grandma."

Face burning, I quickly tried to hide the note back in the folds of the quilt before anyone else could read it. However, judging by the goofy grin on Seth's face as he stood beside me, I think he got a good enough look at it.

Natalie and Sicily's present was great. Apparently tired of hearing me complain about my hair, they gave me a deluxe hair dying kit that included what should have been about a year's supply and hair dye in a kaleidoscope of colors. They were so excited about the gift themselves that they wanted to immediately schedule a hair dying party where all three of us could try out the kit. Thoughtfully, they had also included a gift certificate to an exclusive salon so I could go get my hair fixed after we finished with it.

Unwrapping Wayne's gift, I had trouble not bursting into uncontrollable giggles. He had gotten me the complete set of "Back to the Future" movies. Barely containing my amusement, I did lose it briefly when he leaned down and whispered with wide-eyed innocence, "I thought it might be educational."

Toward the end, my dad awkwardly handed me a large, misshapen package, saying gruffly. "I actually did my own shopping this time, Hannah-girl." Touched, I almost cried at the sight of the wrinkled paper covering the gift. He'd obviously attempted to wrap the gift himself too, and, to me, it was one of the most beautiful things I had ever seen. I had a hard time making myself remove the paper.

Inside was a huge car emergency kit. It included a flashlight that claimed it was bright enough to act as a flare, as well as tools and equipment to fix common vehicle problems. A separate section labeled 'basic survival gear,' included a tarp, rope, blanket, dehydrated food, and first aid kit. All in all, it was the largest, most exhaustive car emergency kit I had ever seen, and I was thrilled.

"I know how you're always nervous about driving," Dad said quietly, looking around to make sure that no one was really listening after the initial gift reveal. "You're such a stickler for safety that I thought you might like this, especially considering what happened when... well, you know. There's also my selfish daddy desire to do whatever I can to keep my little girl safe. If you'd still let me taxi you around, I would."

"Thank you, Dad," I said, wrapping my arms around him and burying my face in his strong, plaid-covered shoulder. "I love it. It's perfect."

Smiling in relief that I actually liked his present, Dad kissed my forehead before gently releasing me.

Waiting until last, Seth showered me with an embarrassing number of presents. Some of the gifts, including a photo album and a pair of silver hoop earrings, I think had been in his cache of gifts he had bought anticipating my return. I was really excited about the high quality art kit he gave me that included everything from watercolors, to acrylics, to oils. In a small jewelry box was another charm for my bracelet.

"It's a little early," Seth said, explaining the little graduation hat charm. "But I figured it was safe to say you were going to pass all your classes." Looking closely, I saw my graduation date engraved on the charm.

This was now the fourth charm for my bracelet. He had already given me a little angel with the date I came back into his life. For Valentine's Day, he'd also given me a little heart charm with both our initials. At this rate, Seth was going to have to buy me a new charm bracelet annually. There are only so many charms one can hold. I thought his thoughtfulness was very sweet though, and I considered the bracelet one of my prized possessions, wearing it always.

As the guests renewed their conversations, I helped clean up the wrapping paper and then followed Seth's mom into the kitchen. Never having known my own mother, I held a sort of fascination for Seth's.

"Thank you for the gift certificate," I told Julie. "Seth must have told you of my favorite clothing store and my recent complaints about my wardrobe."

Julie smiled. "He might have mentioned something about the store. Of course, I like that store too, and I don't know any woman who doesn't complain about her wardrobe on occasion."

"Can I help with anything?" I offered.

"Absolutely not! It's your birthday. Relax. I'm just getting the cake ready to serve."

Lifting the cover, I gaped at the most gorgeous cake I had seen in my life. Delicate, detailed flowers and leaves trailed over the surface of a multilayered cake that would have been fitting for the most extravagant wedding. The flowers and leaves were an unusual black, and, on the white frosting, it created a startling effect reminiscent of the shadows of leaves on the ground. It seemed almost a shame to eat such a work of art let alone mar it by impaling it with the candles Julie had set beside it.

"Don't tell me I'm going to have to blow out twenty-four candles on that cake."

"Seth's orders," Julie confirmed.

"Might as well light the whole cake on fire," I muttered.

"Unfortunately, my Seth is pretty well set in his ways when it comes to... well... just about everything. I've tried to get him to tone down his surprises and his ideas of 'fun,' but it's never worked. You might have better luck than I have, but it seems it might be easier to teach these candles to light themselves than to change Seth McAllister."

"I've definitely run into his Texas-sized stubborn streak," I said.

"Oh, he's not stubborn, he's just..."

"Determined!" we both finished together, laughing.

"I do like your earlier idea about revenge," Julie mused. "I don't know that anyone has ever been able to give him a dose of his own medicine."

"I certainly intend to try."

"I think you can handle him," Julie said playfully looking me up and down as if to size me up. "I think you already have Seth wrapped around your finger."

"I don't know about that. He's not exactly obedient to my wishes. And right here we have Exhibit A," I said, gesturing dramatically to the cake.

"That's a little different. He's trying to make you happy. He just thinks he knows better than you how to do that." Julie's expression turned serious and thoughtful. "I've actually wondered if he's having such a hard time deciding about his career after graduation because he's wanting to make sure he stays close to you."

Surprised, it took me a minute to formulate my thoughts. I knew I needed to ease some of Julie's concerns.

"I know Seth's usually so decisive," I said slowly. "But I don't think his current indecision is because he's trying to cater his plans to mine. Seth knows me by now. He knows that I am the queen of indecision. He can't base his plans on me. I have no idea what I want to be when I grow up!

Seeing Julie smile slightly, I continued to explain. "I've gone ahead and applied to graduate school, but I probably won't know until the morning of the deadline if I'll actually attend. My current thinking is that maybe I could get my Master's degree in Art Restoration. Then I could work someplace like a museum. But, I've also thought about getting my teaching certificate to teach high school art or opening my own gallery. Of course, there is also the dream that I'll become a famous artist and get paid to do what I most love." Dramatically, I sighed and shrugged. "See, Julie, I'm a mess!"

"And Seth knows all this about you?" She questioned, still trying to be serious, even though her eyes were sparkling with laughter at my speech.

"Absolutely! He teases me regularly about my 'Career of the Day.' He knows he can't base a decision on my career because tomorrow I'll probably change my mind. He hasn't even asked my opinion about what offer he should take. He doesn't really discuss it that much. Oh, wait, he did tell me once that he expected me to teach, restore, and create art in my museum / gallery wherever he decided to work next. I said that there were perfectly good planes we could use if we ended up on opposite sides of the country. He said that he supposed he could go ahead and buy his own private jet if need be and fly to see me every few days."

Julie laughed.

"I have no idea why Seth is struggling with this decision, but I'm definitely not the reason," I concluded.

"Okay, I get it. But, I still say that you factor into his decision-making process more than you know. Even if he doesn't ask you your opinion, that doesn't mean he doesn't want to choose something that would allow him to be close to you. He would do anything for you, and you'd never have to even ask. Hannah, I don't think you've quite figured out yet how crazy Seth is about you."

"I know how I feel about him," I said self-consciously. "I'm definitely crazy about him. I just have a hard time imagining Seth could feel the same way about me."

"Hannah, I think you'd better get used to the idea that my son is yours to keep. If you suddenly have an overwhelming desire to go to the moon, Seth will find a way to get you a space shuttle and be your copilot."

"Mom, do you have the cake ready?" Seth called, sticking his head in one of the French doors. "The natives are getting a little restless out here."

Our conversation over, Julie handed me the stack of

plates and forks, while she rushed to grab the cake. "We've been in here yakking, and I completely forgot about the cake!'

I couldn't blow out all twenty-four candles on my cake in one breath, but I hoped that didn't mean that I wouldn't get my birthday wish. As the conversation with Seth's mom replayed through my mind, I hoped she was right in one respect. I wished that the man I was in love with, loved me in return.

After extinguishing the fire hazard, everyone agreed that the cake was delicious, though a bit waxy on top. The cake marked the end of the festivities, and everyone was soon cleaning up and saying their goodbyes. My dad was one of the last guests to leave, and he asked me to walk him out to his car.

Happily, I took his arm and relished even a few minutes of alone time with my Daddy. I had always felt proud that my dad and I were close. We shared a bond that I couldn't really explain. We liked doing things together or just sitting in the living room doing nothing. Dad was my rock growing up. He protected me, comforted me, and was always my biggest fan. Even as an adult, I felt safe and loved when I was around him. Having him give me a hug always felt like coming home.

Nearing his car in the driveway, he stopped.

"I have one other gift for you, Hannah-girl," he said. "It's kind of sentimental, so I didn't really want to give it to you in front of everyone else."

My dad wasn't usually tentative about anything, but, as I opened the small wrapped package he'd handed me, he nervously fiddled with his keys and looked everywhere but at me.

Opening a small velvet jewelry box, I found a tiny heart locket suspended on a delicate gold chain. I had never seen such a small locket. It almost looked as though it should belong to a child. Not given to flamboyant jewelry anyway, I loved the simple necklace the moment I saw it.

"It was your mother's," Dad explained roughly. "The locket doesn't open. It's too tiny. I think your mom must have gotten it when she was a little girl. I don't know for sure, but it was obviously very important to her."

I fingered the necklace almost reverently. Both Abby and I had other things that had been mom's, but I'd never been given something as personal as this. I wondered if Dad had given Abby something like this of Mom's at some point that I just never knew about. But, I certainly wasn't going to ask.

"I had actually intended to give this to you a long time ago," Dad said quietly. "I know your mom would have wanted you to have it. I wish I had a good excuse, but I don't. I completely forgot about it until a few months ago. I'm sorry, Hannah-girl."

"Don't feel bad," I said, turning around so he could help me with the clasp around my neck. "I'm just happy to get it now. I love it. Thank you, Dad. It means a lot to me."

The necklace felt right around my neck. I could tell that I would have a hard time ever taking it off. I didn't care that it might have technically been a child's necklace. I figured it was so tiny and unobtrusive, I could probably wear it with most things and have it not even be noticed. Just reaching up and fingering the tiny gold heart gave me comfort somehow and made me feel a little closer to the mother I never knew.

Feeling tears prick my eyes, I hugged Dad tightly. As I felt his strong arms engulf me and smelled his aftershave, I felt magically transformed into an eight-year old girl who knew she was loved by her daddy. After thanking him for coming to the party and giving me two very special gifts, I waved goodbye to his departing car and walked back into the house.

Staying late and visiting with Seth's parents and Wayne, they insisted that we stay and use their spare bedrooms instead of driving home so late.

"Thank you, Seth," I said at the door to my room. "For everything."

Seth held my hand and squeezed it as if to say, "See, I told you my surprise was good."

I remained quiet too, not quite ready to give him any more encouragement in the surprise department.

My birthday had been wonderful. I couldn't have imagined better. From the friends and family, to the meal, to the gifts, to the cake, everything had seemed perfect. As I finally leaned my head back and closed my eyes in exhaustion, I smiled, remembering the perfect ending to the evening as well. Wayne had gotten his promised chess rematch. The birthday girl had won… twice.

CHAPTER TWELVE

"SETH, would you PLEASE slow down!" We were driving in Seth's BMW to my dad's house the Wednesday after my birthday.

Since Seth had the day off and I'd finished my last final that morning, we were headed to celebrate with Dad. I knew my dad got lonely a lot, so Seth and I tried to spend time with him whenever we could. A lot of people probably wondered why my dad had never remarried. I think in the beginning that he'd been so focused on raising two little girls that he'd never given thought to his own personal life. Now, he claimed he was so cantankerous and set in his ways that he didn't want to go through the retraining involved with a new wife. But, I saw the way he still stared at my mother's picture, and my own conclusion was that, twenty-four years later, he was still very much in love with her.

Both Abby and I tried to relieve Dad's loneliness

whenever possible. Seth was so sweet in that he never seemed to mind having Dad as a tag along. Of course, it's quite possible that I was the tag along. Seth and Dad were good friends in their own right and would feel perfectly comfortable without me around. Today, our modest celebration included helping Dad with some yard work, followed by Chinese takeout and a new release movie.

When Seth immediately put his foot on the brake and slowed after my comment on his speed, I was concerned. It wasn't like him to acquiesce without some remark on either my paranoia or back-seat driving.

"What's wrong, Seth? Are you mad at me?" I quickly reviewed the last week in my mind, trying to figure out if I'd done something he should be upset about. We had both been so busy, we had barely had time to check in with each other since last Saturday. I had been cramming and taking finals while Seth had been trying to finish up some studies and other details of his residency. Coming up with nothing, I pressed, "You haven't said more than three words since you picked me up."

"I'm sorry, Hannah. I'm not upset with you at all. I guess I'm just distracted thinking about Wayne's offer."

"What offer?"

"Didn't I tell you?"

"No. I saw you two talking at my birthday party, but you never mentioned what you'd been talking about."

"I guess we really haven't had a chance to talk since then. I'm sorry. I really thought I had told you." Pausing, Seth ran a hand through his hair, a sure sign that he was agitated about something. "I really need your input on what I should do, Hannah. Wayne is starting a new research company, and he wants me to join him."

"He's doing this instead of accepting one of his we'll-do-anything-to-get-you offers?"

"Yes, and really it sounds ideal. He is partnering with a highly respected older doctor who is at the forefront of a lot of cutting edge research. He also has funding from a wealthy philanthropist who wants to be a silent partner. The company will be completely privately funded and will not be receiving any government grants or funding. This way, he won't have to jump through all the government hoops or have someone looking over his shoulder dictating how something should be done or what he can or can't research. Wayne has a very strong sense of medical ethics and thinks that government funded research isn't necessarily headed in a good direction."

"Forgive me for asking, Seth, but why does Wayne need you? Dr. Wayne Hawkins is like the number one draft pick in the medical field, especially in research, right?"

"His vision for the company is multi-faceted. He wants to be able to fund other worthy research endeavors outside the company as well as do its own research. He needs my skills at this planning stage to figure out how everything can be accomplished. In terms of the company's internal research, he wants me to be in charge of all case studies. Wayne is really good at test tubes and figuring out how a disease should be combated. He's not as skilled with handling patients directly. I am. Wayne's vision includes a facility where people with problems that are difficult to diagnose or treat can come to receive care. It will be the place where people can go when they have nowhere else to turn. He wants me to treat them."

"Wow. I'm not sure how realistic all of that is. But,

you're right, it does sound ideal. What's the problem? Are you nervous about tying your career to Wayne's pie-in-the-sky dream?"

"Yes and no. I have complete confidence in Wayne. No one is more driven or determined than he is. If there is a way for him to get every detail accomplished, he will. Even now, he has plenty of money and people lined up ready to do his bidding."

"Then what's the problem?"

"I'm selfishly worried about me. I'm finished with my residency, but most doctors continue on in specialty training. It's not like education ever ends for a doctor. Wayne claims that the doctor who's partnering with him can continue to teach us. He's promised to teach us everything he knows. Wayne also has an impressive list of other doctors and hospitals that are willing to collaborate with his research and case studies as well as offer any tools or education we may need.

"But," Seth continued, "this isn't the way things are usually done. Wayne and I are both very young in medicine. Just looking at our age and experience, it seems foolhardy to even think about starting our own company. Wayne wants me to be an equal partner in every way. What if I can't handle it? I might not have enough education or be smart enough to deal with the issues we'll face. Added to all this, it does make me nervous that it isn't a sure thing. On the one hand, it could completely fall through and I'd be left with no respect or standing in the medical field. Right now, I have a lot of good offers on the table — offers that would provide me with further training, a secure future, and promised success. On the other hand, this opportunity could be exactly what I've been waiting for — what I've wanted to do my whole life."

I was surprised. I had never seen Seth so unsure about a decision or insecure about his own abilities. He was usually so confident. I had never had to fill the role of encourager. It meant a lot that he trusted me enough to share this part of himself, but I also felt a little daunted that he was expecting my advice or opinion.

After Seth's speech was finished, I sat for a moment collecting my thoughts before speaking. I wanted to say this in a way Seth would understand, but I was not going to make this decision for him.

"Seth, you are an amazingly talented doctor. Your mentors, your peers, everyone has been surprised at your level of knowledge and your natural talent for medicine. They've all said that you are not an ordinary doctor. You told me that Dr. James even said you were ahead of doctors ten years older than you and that he would feel confident recommending you for any position in the country, even his own personal doctor! You are meant to do great extra-ordinary things."

It wasn't lost to me that I was probably the last person who should be giving advice on how to make an important decision. I was the most dysfunctional decision-maker I knew. Even though I'd somehow managed to stick with an Art major long enough to get a degree, I was no closer in deciding what to do next. Seth frequently teased me about having strong opinions on everything except my own future.

Just because I couldn't make a decision didn't mean I wasn't an expert on the underlying theory. Seth listened without comment as I continued my advice. "I don't know what path you should take, Seth. You have to decide that. I just don't think you should base your decision on fear and insecurity. What do you want to do? What opportunity thrills and excites you? Which one do you feel you're supposed to do? What would give you the most satisfaction? Thirty years from now, which one would you regret the least? You're going to be successful and make a difference in the world no matter which way you go."

Seth was silent and still after I finished what I felt was a prize-winning motivational speech. I almost wished someone would've taken notes to direct a version of it back to myself. The only evidence that Seth's brain was even working was his foot's slowly increasing pressure on the gas pedal. Although he had slowed down at my original complaint, he had steadily worked his speed back up. I'm sure it was unconscious, but part of me wondered if he just hoped I wouldn't notice.

Seth finally spoke slowly. "I want to have every opportunity to use my skills to help people and make a difference. It's why I became a doctor." Suddenly, he grinned. It was a bit sheepish, but it also lit up his face like the sun after a storm. "I guess I'm like Wayne. I want the pie in the sky!"

"Well, then," I responded, probably feeling overly proud of myself and my obviously good advice. "I guess you have your answer." If only I could follow my own advice and make a decision as easily as Seth.

Pausing for a beat, I decided I couldn't stand it any longer. "And don't think I haven't noticed your speed. You're going faster now than you were before!"

"Hey! You know the rules! No backseat driving!" Seth's usual good mood had returned, chasing off any previous unquestioning obedience. "You could have driven today, but you didn't want to."

"My SUV is overdue for an oil change! Forget the rules! I can't just sit back while you get us killed with your need for speed. You'll do Wayne absolutely no good if you're dead!"

"Like I said, you could have driven, but you chose not to. So, sit tight and let me drive."

I sighed heavily and folded my arms across my chest with annoyance. Seth and I had an agreement, mostly due to my phobias, that the owner of the car we took was always the driver. Furthermore, the passenger was not allowed to criticize the driving. For the most part, the arrangement worked very well. Seth was a good driver and was usually extra careful because he knew how paranoid I was. However, sometimes my fear got the best of me.

Now, he wasn't exactly going over the speed limit, but we were no longer on the freeway and the road was very curvy. I would have been more comfortable with at least 10 mph shaved off. Seeing that he wasn't slowing down at all, I knew my nerves and mouth would get the best of me soon. Leaning my head back, I closed my eyes, trying to tell myself that Seth was a good driver, and I should trust him.

The eyes-closed technique was one I frequently used when feeling traumatized by Seth's driving. Deep down, I knew the problem was more mine than his. I'd found if I closed my eyes and tried to activate my imagination, my mind didn't register the sights that made me afraid. Also, I figured that if I was going to die in a car accident, I'd rather not see it anyway.

"I'm sorry, Hannah," Seth said contritely, reaching over and touching the back of my hand. "Open your eyes. I'll slow down. It's only 1:00 now. There's no hurry to get to your dad's. Here you were so nice and supportive of me, and

I'm being insensitive to you. I sometimes forget how hard it is for you to let other people drive."

"It's not just other people. It's even hard for me to let *me* drive!"

Seeing that Seth had indeed slowed down, I felt immediate anxiety relief, followed by a sharp pang of guilt.

"I'm the one who's sorry, Seth. I know you're a good driver, and you weren't going too fast. I'm just a freak."

"You aren't a freak, Hannah. You just helped me make a very important decision, and just last week, you won my parents over. They think you're wonderful. They didn't even mention the word 'freak.'"

"What do you mean, I 'won them over,'" I asked suspiciously. "You told me before my birthday that they liked me. What did I win them over from?"

Seth's expression looked awkward, like he'd let slip something he'd never intended to reveal. "They did like you. They just had some... reservations before they met you. Now they couldn't be happier. They think you're perfect for me."

"What reservations?"

"They were just a little worried about our age difference. I think Mom was afraid you'd be some meek little girl who did everything I said and kowtowed to my rather strong opinions on everything."

There's no other way to describe it: I snorted.

Seth smiled, his eyes were focused on the road but dancing merrily. "Obviously, that's not the case. Mom was able to figure that out right away. I think you completely won her over right away when you apologized because you were going to be seeking a 'very serious and nasty revenge' on her son."

It's not like I hadn't been insecure about the difference in our ages before. It was yet another reason I was mystified about Seth's interest in me. Chewing my lower lip worriedly, I asked Seth himself, "You're not concerned about the difference in our ages?"

"No, not at all! We were a lot closer in age when we first met five and a half years ago, but my thirty to your twenty-four isn't that much. You're very mature, and I tend to be immature," he said with a wink. "I think we probably average out to be about the same."

I looked out the window, trying to mask my insecurities by feigning interest as we entered the outskirts of my hometown. Interpreting my silence to mean that I wasn't convinced, Seth continued. "Hannah, I don't care how old you are. I wouldn't even care if you were seven years older than me. It's you I waited for; it's you I want."

Still watching the passing scenery, I protested softly, "But your parents…"

"My parents don't even care about the age issue now," Seth interrupted. "Mom has always thought I needed to have a strong woman. She told me after meeting you that she thought you would do a more than adequate job of challenging and keeping me on my toes."

"What about your dad? Did he like me?"

Seth smiled sheepishly. "Dad told me not to foul things up and let you get away."

I laughed, feeling slightly better about the situation. "What did you say?"

"I told him I had no intention of letting you get away… for any reason." Seth's expression suddenly turned serious and lines creased his smooth forehead. Not knowing what had brought the sudden change, I waited. By the look on his face, I knew it was only a matter of time before he gathered his thoughts enough to tell me what was bothering him. Seth was an open book and not the type to leave anything unsaid.

"That's why you still need to go get checked out, Hannah," Seth finally concluded.

"Seth, don't even start!" I retorted, instantly angry. Usually appreciative of Seth's honest communication, I would have much rather he'd kept these thoughts to himself. I was so tired of him continually bringing this subject up. "Nothing has happened in the last five months! I feel fine. I'm obviously healthy. Just let it go!"

"I can't. You time traveled twice. The second time we almost had to take you to the hospital. Don't you understand? I need to do something! I can't just wait until it happens again."

"It won't!"

"You don't know that! I can't handle turning around one day and finding you gone again. Then, if you even make it back to this time, I can't handle watching you suffer and possibly die because of the trauma time traveling did to your body."

"Fine! What do you expect me to do, Seth? Consent to be a lab rat? Possibly be sent to a psychiatric facility because who in their right mind would even believe me?"

"No! Just let me run a few tests. Look at your medical records. Make sure there isn't anything obvious out of the ordinary. When was the last time you even went to the doctor for a checkup?"

"Turn left here."

"What?"

"TURN LEFT HERE!"

At the last second, Seth obediently turned into the parking lot.

"What's going on, Hannah!" Seth said, his own eyes now furious. "You could have caused an accident with your yelling."

"You mentioned medical records. This is the hospital where I was born. The family physician I've seen since I was a child also has his office in the rear wing of the hospital."

Understanding dawned in Seth's eyes. "We can get your medical records?"

"I'm tired of fighting with you about this. Maybe if we compromise, you'll leave me alone. I'm not consenting to any tests, but, if you want my medical records, they're yours. That way, maybe you'll believe that I have an excellent health history and there's nothing to worry about."

Without replying, Seth hopped out of the car and came to my side. "Thank you, Hannah," he said, his voice still a little stiff from being so angry.

Walking toward the single level, orange brick hospital, I adopted the role of tour guide, hoping to further diffuse the tension by talking about a subject neither one of us really cared about.

"The hospital is still pretty small, but it's bigger than when I was a child. They've since added the wing of doctor's offices at the back." Getting no response from Seth, I continued. "When I was young, they didn't even have full time doctors on site. If there was an emergency, they would have to page the doctor on call, who could be across town doing who knows what. I remember breaking my arm when I was about seven and having to wait for an hour in the emergency room before a doctor showed up."

We walked through the automatic doors and into the tiled reception area. Not needing directions to the office wing, I led the way to the left and down a hallway. Still receiving no response from Seth, I decided to wow him with my knowledge of local history. "The hospital is actually a historic landmark in the town. The original brick building was built in..."

"Hannah, I don't care."

"What?" I said, stopping in the hallway and staring at the man who had shocked me with his rudeness.

"I... don't... care!" Seth repeated, enunciating carefully.

My fury resumed its trip on the escalator as Seth continued.

"I'd rather discuss something I do care about – you. Just to let you know, this isn't a compromise. I'm not letting you off the hook. I'm happy about getting your medical records, but you WILL let me do a few medical tests as well."

"No, I won't!" My brain, muddled with anger at his audacity, tried to sift through a variety of appropriate responses. I wanted to stamp my foot and shout phrases like: 'You can't make me!' and 'You're not the boss of me!" But I thought the childishness of it might weaken my case.

"Hannah, I'm telling you this is important to me. I'm not going to let it go."

I couldn't remember ever being so angry with Seth. "And I'm telling you to BACK OFF!"

Seth ran a hand through his hair in obvious frustration, then looked at me, his eyes angry and smoldering. Staring hard at him, I saw a subtle change in his eyes right before he pushed me into a small alcove at the side of the hallway.

"What do you think you're…!"

His lips were on mine before I could finish my complaint. It wasn't a gentle kiss, but it wasn't cruel either. It seemed as if Seth channeled all of his frustration and anger into the kiss and the result was passion. All of my own anger suddenly vanished, leaving me weak in his arms. My hands lifted and tangled in his hair. My breathing grew ragged and my heart felt like it would beat out of my chest. Seth had never kissed me like that before. I was both afraid that he'd stop and afraid that he'd continue. I'd never felt such waves of emotion as his lips moved hungrily over mine.

As suddenly as he started, Seth stopped kissing me, pulled away a few inches and looked into my eyes. His hands moved to cup my face gently.

"Hannah, I love you. I love you so much that those three words seem inadequate to express what I really feel. I can't bear the thought of losing you. I can't do it! I'm not willing to risk it! Hannah, would you please let me run some tests? If for no other reason than to make the man who's crazy in love with you feel a little better? Would you please do it for me?

I felt a physical pain in my chest as my heart seemed to race and ache at the same time. Seth loved me! Like the blind being raised on a window, I suddenly realized that it was Seth's love and passion for me that fueled his anger and frustration over the testing. Tears pricked my eyes as I realized how selfish and insensitive I'd been.

Looking up with watery eyes, I smiled hesitantly. "Well, when you put it that way… I'll do whatever testing you want done, Seth." My smile changing to be a little teasing, I added, "I just don't know why you didn't explain it that way a long time ago. It sure would have saved us a lot of trouble!"

Seth chuckled, then showered gentled kisses on my eyes, cheeks, nose, and neck. I had trouble forming any coherent thoughts or even remembering why I'd been mad at him in the first place.

"By the way," I whispered. "I'll only do the tests because I love you too."

Stopping and lifting his head, Seth looked at me with a silly grin on his face and joy dancing in his blue-green eyes. Taking a deep, shuddering breath, kissing my forehead, and releasing me, Seth stepped back.

"If I kiss you again like I want to, Hannah, we will never make it to get those medical records."

"Rain check?" I asked, entwining my hand with his and stepping out of the alcove.

"Not sure," he replied. "I think you might be dangerous. Feeling what you make me feel has got to be hazardous to my health."

Rounding the corner of the hallway to the medical offices, I stopped mid-stride.

"What's wrong?" Seth asked, concerned.

I pointed. "The medical offices should be right there."

Instead of a hallway that opened up to a reception area surrounded by doctors' offices, I was pointing to a solid wall.

I turned around in a full circle. I had an awful sinking feeling in the pit of my stomach as I began to notice other differences. The paint on the walls looked dingy, the tile old, and the pictures on the wall cheap.

"Seth, none of this is right," I mumbled, nervously fingering Mom's locket clasped around my neck.

The feeling of dread was rapidly transforming into panic. Nothing was as it should be.

Then I knew.

My mind swirled with everything that had just happened. My eyes swung to Seth's confused gaze and locked. In that instant, I knew two things. The man I loved, loved me back. And, wherever, *whenever* I was, he had come with me.

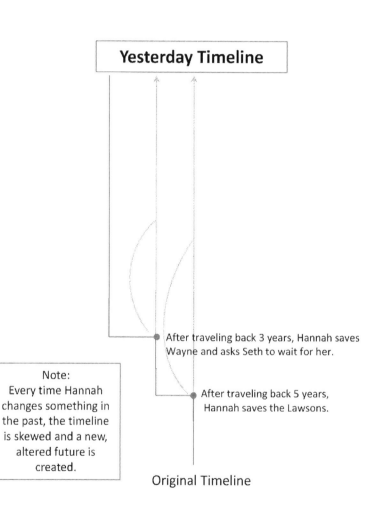

Yesterday Timeline

After traveling back 3 years, Hannah saves Wayne and asks Seth to wait for her.

Note:
Every time Hannah changes something in the past, the timeline is skewed and a new, altered future is created.

After traveling back 5 years, Hannah saves the Lawsons.

Original Timeline

READER'S GUIDE

YOU may have noticed that in the dedication at the beginning of this book, I reference Psalm 139. While the *Yesterday* series is a fantastic set of stories filled with twists and excitement, it is also intended as an illustration of this psalm.

As you read this book, did you think about how God is working in your own life? Did you consider how He has a purpose for you and a person He wants you to become? My prayer is that you did.

The story line is meant as an extraordinary example of the way God works in our lives to accomplish His purpose and mold us into He wants us to be.

One of the most amazing things to me is that I wrote the dedication for this book prior to conceiving Hannah's full story which unfolds throughout the entirety of the *Yesterday* series. In fact, I pretty much forgot I had included that psalm until one day when I was working on book 5. As I was trying to think of a verse that would really tie Hannah's life and the series together, I suddenly remembered referencing a verse in book 1. I went back and looked. Then tears came to my eyes.

While I didn't know Hannah's full story or what it would mean when I started writing this series, God did. He also probably knew that if He had given me the full idea right away, I would have run the other direction! But, as in Hannah's life, God had a plan from before time began. He has a plan for me and this story, and He has a plan for you.

My hope and prayer is that in reading this series, you will enjoy and love it, but also gain a deeper understanding of how wonderful, good, and perfect God's plans are for you. After all, Hannah's story is patterned from a real God who loves you enough to plan and orchestrate your life in such a way to glorify Him and bring about your greatest good.

May these questions and your discussion bless you in your relationship with God. Please search scripture, carefully consider, and pray. May the Lord draw you close to Him and give you the wonderful assurance of His love and purpose He has for you.

> Your eyes saw my substance, being yet unformed. And in Your book they all were written, the days fashioned for me, when as yet there were none of them.
> Psalm 139:16 (NKJV)

When facing the seemingly impossible task of saving the Lawson family, Hannah turned to God for help.

1. Would you have handled things as Hannah did if encountering a similar situation? How do you react when facing a crisis? What promises in the Bible would help you know that you will have courage and strength when needed? *Matthew 28:18*

2. When facing stressful situations, what is your default reaction? Do you think to pray? How can you prepare for the tough times in a way that will make prayer a priority? *Ephesians 6:17-18, Phillipians 4:6-7*

Hannah attributes her time traveling to a miracle, that she was sent to save the Lawsons as part of God's plan.

3. Do you think God still does miracles today? Have you witnessed any miracles?

4. What about the less obvious kind of miracles? Can you think of times when you've been in the right

place at the right time to help someone or be an instrument of God's plan? *Ephesians 2:10*

When Hannah time travels a second time, she makes two significant changes to the timeline. Later she wonders about the ethics of those actions.

5. What do you think? Should Hannah have preserved the timeline by staying out of it and letting Wayne take the blame for someone else's sin?

6. Should she have sent the note for Seth to wait for her even though she knew it would change the lives of others?

7. Is it sometimes difficult to figure out right from wrong or is everything always black and white? What ethical decisions (in work, financial, personal life, etc.) have you struggled with? *James 1:5, James 1:21-22*

One of Seth's theories is that God was able to use even Hannah's selfishness, her sins, to accomplish His Will.

8. What do you think of this idea? Is God able to redeem even our mistakes for our good? *Romans*

5:20b-21, Romans 8:28

9. Tell of a time when you feel God brought good out of your mistakes.

Though she doesn't understand why or how, Hannah believes God has used her time traveling as part of His plan.

10. Are you currently in a situation where you think God might be using you toward a specific purpose? Maybe you have an opportunity as a witness, friend, or servant. Please share and pray with one another that God will accomplish His purpose for His glory and your good.

If you used this guide for a group discussion, before closing in prayer, please read all of *Psalm 139*.

NOTES:

_____

_____

_____

_____

_____

_____

_____

_____

_____

_____

_____

_____

_____

YESTERDAY SERIES

The Yesterday Series:

Book 1: Yesterday

Book 2: The Locket

Book 3: Today

Book 4: The Choice

Book 5: Tomorrow

Book 6: The Promise

FIND all the stories in the *Yesterday* series wherever fine books are sold.

MORE GREAT BOOKS

The Tru Exceptions Series:

Book 1: Baggage Claim

Book 2: Point of Origin

Book 3: Mirage

Stand-Alone Novels:

Secret Santa

The Romance of the Sugar Plum Fairy

Random Acts of Cupid

The Assumption of Guilt

SNEAK PEEK

ENJOY this special excerpt from *The Locket*, book 2 in the *Yesterday* series, available now wherever fine books are sold.

I immediately started trembling from head to toe. This could not be happening! Not again!

Just two minutes ago I'd been stealing a few minutes in Seth's arms. He'd told me he loved me. We'd been on our way to pick up my medical records from the offices in the Jackson hospital. We walked down the hall and now faced a solid wall that shouldn't be there.

I closed my eyes, trying to breathe deeply. The decor was wrong, the layout was wrong, everything about the hospital wasn't as I clearly remembered.

And I knew. This had happened before.

Seth didn't know. Not yet. It's not like my boyfriend had ever experienced this with me before. But this was the third time in my life I'd turned around to find everything different from mere seconds before.

There was only one explanation. I had time traveled again.

But there was one change this time. I opened my eyes and looked at Seth. This was the first time someone else was experiencing the same thing I was.

I needed to tell him. But I didn't want to.

"Seth, the office wing should be right here!" I said hoarsely.

"Maybe you just remembered wrong," Seth said. "We can find someone and ask directions."

"No, I'm not remembering wrong," I said. "I've been going to see my doctor here since I was ten. The office wing of the hospital should be right where that wall is."

"Here, let's go ask someone."

He practically dragged me down the hallway. He didn't understand. How could he? As we turned right and followed the hallway, I had the strongest urge to cover my eyes. Nausea rushed over me in a wave.

I didn't want to see anymore! Every step, every dated object I saw confirmed what I already knew. This was not our time.

"Seth, everything is wrong," I whispered, too terrified to mention the true thoughts stampeding through my head. If I didn't say it out loud, maybe it wouldn't be true.

Seth didn't seem to hear me. Instead, he focused on a

couple of young nurses having a heated discussion at an intersection in the hallway.

"We're moving her into the delivery room," the nurse with frizzy blond hair said. To my frantic, overactive mind, she resembled a rock star in a music video from the eighties.

"The doctor isn't even here!" said the other nurse, who had straight black hair and heavy makeup. She reminded me of a fortune teller. Her large hoop earrings only completed the effect.

"We don't have a choice. She's not doing well. I don't know what else to do. We can't get a hold of the doctor. He isn't responding to his pager. We'll just have to get everything prepared so he can just do the delivery when he gets here."

The blond rocker nurse turned quickly and left. Seth and I moved forward to talk to the other one. Before Seth could even form a question, the rocker nurse was back, pushing the bed of a pregnant woman who was obviously in hard labor. A man, probably her husband, trailed behind.

As the woman was pushed past, she turned her tired, sweat-soaked face and looked our direction.

I felt all of the blood drain from my face. I tried to breathe, but only a strangled sound came out of my throat. Feeling like I was going to pass out, I grabbed at Seth.

"Hannah, what's wrong? What is it?"

Finally, getting a little air, I whispered past my constricting throat. "Seth, that woman! She's my mother!"

ABOUT THE AUTHOR

AMANDA TRU loves to write exciting books with plenty of unexpected twists. She figures she loses so much sleep writing the things, it's only fair she makes readers lose sleep with books they can't put down!

Amanda has always loved reading, and writing books has been a lifelong dream. A vivid imagination helps her write captivating stories in a wide variety of genres. Her current book list includes everything from holiday romances, to action-packed suspense, to a Christian time travel / romance series.

Amanda is a former elementary school teacher who now spends her days being mommy to three little boys and her nights furiously writing. Amanda and her family live in a small Idaho town where the number of cows outnumber the number of people.

Connect with Amanda Tru online: http://amandatru.blogspot.com/

CONNECT ONLINE

Author site:

http://amandatru.blogspot.com/

Newsletter email sign up:

http://eepurl.com/ZQdw9

Facebook:

https://www.facebook.com/amandatru.author

Twitter:

https://twitter.com/TruAmanda

GooglePlus+:

https://plus.google.com/+AmandaTru

Pinterest:

http://www.pinterest.com/truamanda/

Goodreads:

https://www.goodreads.com/author/show/5374686.Amanda_Tru

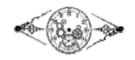

Made in the USA
Lexington, KY
22 April 2016